du Lac

ALAN RICHARDSON

SKYLIGHT
PRESS

First published in Great Britain in 2014 by Skylight Press,
210 Brooklyn Road, Cheltenham, Glos GL51 8EA

Designed and typeset by Rebsie Fairholm
Publisher: Daniel Staniforth
Cover photography by Rebsie Fairholm using texture art by Sascha Duensing.

www.skylightpress.co.uk

Printed and bound in Great Britain by Lightning Source, Milton Keynes.

British Library Cataloguing in Publication Data:
A catalogue record for this book is available from the British Library.

ISBN 978-1-908011-95-4

To
my lovely wayward friends Clare and Raine Cully, who were
duLacquered before anyone, and have helped bring him through,
and Sue Kearley, who knows what it's like to be away with the
faeries...

my wife Margaret, who has her own brand of High Magick and
has regularly stopped me getting pixie-led on remote mountain-
tops. Not all of them physical.

Myth is not a no thing, an insubstantial conceptual
will o' the wisp. It is coded into the cells and waters,
the seas, of the unconscious. It dwells in our little finger
and plays along the spine as well as the spirit. It grants
us access to the DNA of the human psyche, the source
patterns originating in the ground of our being. It gives
us the key to our personal and historical existence.
Without mythic keys... we would only have a grey world,
with little if anything calling us forward to that strange
and beautiful country that recedes even as we attempt to
civilize it.
Jean Houston

WARNING

I don't know who or what du Lac is but I feel it might be wise to use the pronoun 'he' rather than 'it'.

He first came into my head when I was about 7. I was no infant prodigy so I must have been reading a simple book about the Knights of the Round Table. It was not the jousting, derring-do and sword-play which struck me but the few paragraphs about the chaste Galahad and Perceval attaining the Holy Grail while Lancelot of the Lake had to stand outside and watch.

I had an intuitive understanding of this Holy Grail thing but the word 'chaste' was a new one. I asked my Mam what it meant but she gave me a funny look and made me go and wash behind my ears.

Although I could thrum to the splendour of the Grail experience this was overshadowed by the indefinable sense of injustice that I felt with regard to du Lac. It left me with a kind of controlled sadness, always pulling back from a certain despair. It never quite went away.

He burst into my consciousness again some 30 years later with some power – perhaps because I knew only too well what the word 'chaste' meant by then. I felt compelled to write an essay 'The Depths of the Lake' which attempted to put across his viewpoint. It has been reprinted in various journals many times since.

Although I have modified/evolved/changed my opinions completely about many things in the esoteric field over several decades, I am still certain about this: if du Lac was denied heaven because he wasn't chaste, because he had loved too much and unwisely and done stupid things for love, then the Holy Grail itself and the Heaven it offered was not worth a spit.

I don't know whether du Lac is a wild ancestral faery being, a magickal current using a human image to express itself, an historical member of the del Acqs family, or an archetype resonating to various tetchy aspects of my own personality. Or perhaps bits and pieces of all these.

But when he came galloping into my psyche again in the summer of 2013 during a walking holiday in the Isle of Wight, I had no choice but to agree to tell his story. I did warn him that my version would be very different to what he might want: his light would be filtered through the lens of my own character and thus filled with my quirks, concerns, gross immaturity, quasi-learning and probably tinged with madness.

He didn't seem too worried. I think he was glad to get his armour off. Plus he was quite insistent that I didn't call him 'Lancelot'. As I found later, when I studied the earliest sources telling his story, this was never his birth-name.

If this book should awaken the spirit of the great du Lac within the reader, then I accept no responsibility for the havoc he might cause.

Alan Richardson
Wiltshire

The Once and Future King? No – the eternal arse. That should have been his *true* name: Arser, rather than Arthur. Truly, he became witless. Mounted his sister. Plus some other women whose names escape me. Could not get it up for a real woman like my Gwenevere. Then there was that dickless wonder the Fisher King, acting like a pimp toward the Round Table Gang. Which was the biggest bunch of pompous, po-faced, precious little mummy's boys you have ever seen. Why did they need so much armour? Wimps. I hammered them all.

As for their precious Holy Grail: it stank, contained two dead fish, mouth to tail. I would rather have a bowl of Tupperware. Believe me I saw it close enough. And if I never see the dreary marshes of Avalon again, with all of its high priestesses smudging their ways up the high street of Glastonbury to find renewal amid the broad sunlit uplands of the Job Centre on their way to the Pleaides, then it will be too soon.

I will not have a word said against Gwenevere. I will cut open anyone who does and give a twist with the blade so their intestines fall out. I will do that even though knives are banned on the streets of Britain and my native Gaul today. Rightly so for those who were not bred to use such things.

King Arser… Forgive me, I may be crass in my rage but I am not vulgar. It was that fat guy the Merlin who told me that was Arthur's real name: *Asar*. The Green King. The Horned One from the Old Land of Egypt. Whom the Greeks later called Osiris. I make no judgement, but will you tell you strange truths in due course. After what he became in his later days, he will always be Arser to me.

People go dewy eyed when they think of him, even though they know that his grave in that Abbey is a fake. They dream about him asleep under a hill somewhere, waiting for the call to defend Britain at its direst hour, when him and his knights will come galloping out, all pennons flying, rubbing the sleep from their eyes and making sure their swords are loose in their scabbards.

Here is a secret. He is not asleep. He is wide awake and scared. Always. It is me who does the business. Still. Arser just lies there, blinking slowly, almost crapping himself but not quite. I used to love him.

Who the hell do you think you are?! you are asking. You have to ask that, because you follow those morons Malory, Geoffrey of Monmouth, the mealy-mouthed prig von Eschenbach and the cretinous Chrétien de Troyes. (Who, *bien sûr*, knew more than he dared say about us *fées* or fays or Faeries, largely because I told him during one drunken night.) You follow them like sheep. You cannot think for yourself. You think holiness has to be nice, *très jolie*. You think God prefers reverence, manners and good breeding. You want the women in the Arseriad to be ethereal, genteel, obedient little blonde spirits in see-through dresses and no body hair. Yet I know that the real wenches would rip your balls off as soon as look at you, and juggle them in the air while crying *Houp-là!*

I will tell you who I am. I am the one the women all used to dream about – really love – when Arser was still trying to get his first, petit erection. I am the one who taught the world how to fight and how to be passionate. I'm the one that half the boys on the planet wanted to be like when they grew up, while the other half – the bad ones and little shits – woke sweating and shaking from their night terrors, screaming my name:

du Lac.

I had to surface last week. Friday it was. I think. It was in all the journals. I surfaced because a woman needed rescuing. And despite the later fanfare – which I hate – I was rewarded with a glimpse of my elusive Gwenevere – or Jenny as the English say the name these days – nodding approval during the fight and then slipping off into the shadows before I could reach her.

It was late. Midway between Compline and Matins, I feel. The inns of the town had long closed. I was sitting on a bench in the bare, flat stone expanse from which an Abbey rises like an iceberg. In a town known as Bath. In the realm that used to be Logres but is now, they tell me, England. A mere step away from my homeland of Brittany. I liked the way the great towers of the abbey seemed to sway against the starlit night sky, like fronds in a fish-tank, the thin ghostly clouds swimming by. Carved in the grey-gold stone of these are ladders which show little angels climbing up toward their god. One of the angels, nearer the top, is shown falling off. Perhaps, like me, he was denied heaven because he was not chaste. I like that one.

There had been rain. Warm, soft. Lights reflected across the shallow puddles. Behind me I had a sense of the hot mineral waters of the Roman Baths, which nudged against me like an old cat. Purring.

A young woman walked past. I could tell by her gait she was a Faery trapped uneasily in human form. Making the best of it as so many of us do. She was pear-shaped, wore tight black leggings and a sort of black vest. Her moon-shaped face was shining, and her hair was a single red strip. Mohican.

She smiled at me and went on past, her flip-flops making slapping noises on the stone.

Enchanté, I said softly, and meant it. I was taught by my foster mother, the Lady of the Lake, that all women, no matter how old or young, how fat or skinny, are creatures of delight and beauty and should be treated as such. It is advice – no a command – that has served me well through the ages. At that moment a group of young men turned sharply around the corner and into her path. Drunk. Vulgar. Heavily tattooed.

I have nothing against tattoos, you understand. Have ancient ones of my own. The stories told on the arms, chests, faces of those men were disgusting.

Woo-hoo said one of them when he saw la fille.

Miss Wibbly-wobbly! Like one a them toys you can't push over! shouted another, and tried to do so. There were only three of them. I wished there had been more.

They did not see me. But they felt that cold wind which always springs up when I become Who I am.

I walked toward them.

Uh-oh – here's another one! Must be her dad!

When a woman is in distress I am every woman's dad.

Arrêtez I said softly, for they were pushing her around within their triangle.The leader – and I can always tell the natural leader within any gang – turned to face me. Mistake. Big mistake. It gives me a greater target.

I hate Romanians he said.

I took a deep breath. I had been trying, with the Merlin's help, to learn and express tolerance. Forgiveness, even, although in my mind the verb 'to forgive' means the same as 'to condone', and some things a warrior can never condone.

Let her go. Say sorry. Dites désolé.

They did not need to say anything, it was all in the alcoholes of their eyes.

My kind see objects in a way that pure humans do not. I can look at a mantel clock and see the dial and hands. I can also see the bits behind which wind and adjust, and also the dirt. I can see far to the right and the left without turning my head. So when I looked at the leader I looked at him hard. I let him see Who I was. He frowned. Looked surprised. His mouth opened as if to say sorry. Perhaps. Picture the three apes, standing before me, the sweet girl behind them too afraid to run.

I never took my gaze from the middle one, with red hair, transfixing him. Then with the first and fourth fingers of my right hand, I jabbed into the exact centres of the eyeballs of the ape on my right. At the same moment, *exactement*, I stabbed the middle finger of my left hand into that little dip below the Adam's apple of the primate on my left.

One could not see. The other no longer speak. See no evil. Speak no evil. Two down.

Without moving my gaze from the leader I curved both my hands and (with only a portion of my supernatural strength) clapped them to his ears – *BOF!* – the air pockets in my palms bursting his ear drums. Hear no evil. It all took a second. Less.

They writhed on the ground. I offered the girl my arm and walked her away from the havoc. Gave her money for a taxi home. Five English pounds.

Oo are you? she asked, shyly, but with wonder.

I am the great du Lac, I said with a sudden grin.

This was not because I had been gallant. I am always gallant. Nor because I had hospitalised three Bad People. It was because in the shadows, and disappearing into the night in her own uncatchable way, I had caught a glimpse of Gwenevere again.

I think she nodded her approval. I am sure I heard her laugh. A Faery's laugh.

The girl went to the police, and then the papers. The whole thing was captured on this thing they have called CCTV, though the picture was very grainy and no-one could identify me. It just looked like I had waved my hands before them, like a conductor. The thugs themselves, *evidement*, wanted to sue for assault. They had just been havin a laff, they said. Meant no harm. Innit. Then this lunatic attacked them.

The girl knew better. The common folk knew better. The Good People of Bath were pleased that they had a mysterious champion in their midst. Rewards were offered for my identity.

What name did he give, they asked her on the local news.

'*e said he was, er, er… Dulux.*

Like the paint?

She nodded.

I smiled. Perhaps I should call myself Matt, or even Gloss in future. They are names with nice textures to them. Anything is better than Lancelot.

One small part of me is probably 45, if you count in linear terms. Or is it 35? I only do that to silence the fat Merlin who still tries to tell me what I should and should not be doing in The Plan, the Pattern. Merde! I am not sure how old I am. When I was born – *where* I was born – they did not have birth certificates. They did not have paper, or writing, and as far as I can recall they all communicated without words. So I'm probably a hundred times that age when I've had a few human beers and start dancing on the pin-head along with the numberless tipsy angels.

No I am not Ahasuerus, the so-called Wandering Jew who is doomed to walk the earth for an eternity. I have met him a few times but try to hide when I hear his heavy chains of guilt clanking along the road. What a moaner.

Nor am I the Comte de Saint-Germain, who stumbled upon the Philosopher's Stone and learned to avoid Death. He started off as a bejewelled pansy in the French courts and only got worse as the centuries followed. Tried to sell me recipes for removing wrinkles and dyeing hair before he saw my reflection in a pond and realised Who I am. The cold wind sprang up, rippling my reflection and making his diamonds rattle.

Du Lac! Mon Dieu! he said, bowing. I put my hand on his periwig and forced him to continue his bow so that his face was pushed into the ground at my feet. I am not anyone's dieu.

I was about to walk away but he spat the earth from his mouth, rose to his knees like a supplicant, straightened his wig and hissed:

I have a message from Gwenevere.

I lifted him to his feet with a single hand. Slapped him, but gently. Immortals do not feel pain like you humans. He quite enjoyed it. I stopped.

She said that she will meet you at the Place of Waters.

What Place of Waters? Where?

He shrugged.

When?

M'sieur… We eternals… We never know what day or even century it is. I tell you all that I know.

He was speaking truth. There was nothing more to be slapped out of him. As I walked away, intending to have another look at some ponds and fountains in the forest of Brocéliande, and perhaps some frantic but invariably tedious sex with Morgana, he called after me:

M'sieur du Lac…Sir, chevalier…when I was a boy, I dreamed of being like you.

I looked at him pityingly.

Zut! You could not bear love's pain.

Perhaps something of Ahasuerus has rubbed off on me in passing, because I have wandered this watery earth since, miserable, looking for the true Place of Waters where I might find my love.

So I cannot say for sure how old I am because I cannot see my beginnings. When I try to look, I'm peering into the lake bottom which is my genesis: things are stirred up, rising like muddy, formless wraiths that soon dissolve back into the dark, cold waters. There is a pressure in those depths on my eyeballs which makes my vision not true. Strong currents. Things touch me: debris? rotting vegetation? old loves? mouldering corpses? memories of my creation? It is deep, deep water and yet I can breathe it as well as air.

That is why I am 'du Lac'. Of the lake. Or rather of *the* Lake. I will tell you where it is. Later. You might be surprised. It was there that I began, or was begat, and where I must return one day if I can clear it of the debris.

The Lake is why I walk the way I do: left foot forward; transfer all weight; then – and only then – lift right foot and put it forward; transfer weight. Try it. Clumsy? If one foot lifts before a full transfer of weight, there is a danger of me soaring into the air. Though I have not done that for an exceedingly long time – even in linear terms. Imagine, the pure humans among you, how odd and difficult it is to try and walk along the bottom of a swimming pool as you would on land. Me, I can walk fast like this. I stamp across the world. I always have weight and power to draw upon. Like all good fighters, I am never unbalanced. Truly.

I must be getting old. Somehow. I, who was often teased and challenged by Gwenevere to keep vigil for three days and nights at a stretch and watch over her precious hawk, ready to be *en garde* at a moment's notice, have little patience. I was sitting in the café of the Pump Rooms, which are next to the Abbey and part of the Roman Baths themselves. The vast room where they eat and drink and do the tarantella on wild occasions has pale yellow walls like solid sunlight, huge windows that turn silver in the noonday sun, and chandeliers by which a previous age is hooked and left dangling, like a great fish. So it is also right next to a Place of Waters where I hoped to find Gwenevere. God knows I have been to many such.

A string trio was playing. Two men and a girl. Their notes were like ripples on a pond. Most pleasing – if my heart had not been pounding with anticipation. Then Sir Bruce appeared. Sir Bruce sans Pitié. My enemy. If I am born of earth and water, he is a creature of air and fire. I despise him. We have fought throughout the ages. He always escapes before the final blow. Or he begs for mercy under the system of chivalry that binds me. He says we need each other. He says we are of a kind. Jamais!

Pax? he said to me, holding up his empty hands to show that he held no weapons. Yet he knew that du Lac would never fight in a place like this.

Pax, I said begrudgingly. Had been through this before. Often.

He is not of my kind. He has silver-grey hair swept at either side of his brow like the wings of a gannet. A cheap suit with a pale blue shirt and ridiculous yellow tie. Brown shoes, no socks. I could cope with his violence, but his *gaucherie* was a crime against humanity.

As he started to speak a thin woman interrupted him. Her hair was wild, she wore reflecting sunglasses. Vaguely familiar but also frantic. Nervous. She was almost doing a tap-dance on the polished floor.[1]

Dr McHaffee, I need you to –

He shushed her. His finger on her lips. Had he been cruel I would have struck, place of sanctuary or not. She shushed, but looked at him with hurt in her eyes. I knew that because I could see behind the mirrors. Why are human women attracted to men of cruelty and control?

Miss Macleod… please, tonight, at my office, 5 o' clock. You know the agreement. Not now.

She might have argued – she was clearly used to arguing – but she saw me. I do not think she saw Who I am, but she saw the astral equivalent of a sign on my chest which said Danger of Death. She hesitated, teetered, nodded, and walked away.

Michael he said to me. He called me that. Perverse.

Sir Bruce sans Pitié I replied.

He laughed. A very human laugh. It sounded like a cormorant choking on its catch. Men who have no sense of irony laugh like this. Loudly.

Is that who I am now? Sir Bruce? Without pity did you say? Where did that come from?

I said nothing. Rien. Sir Bruce was always good with swords (though never in my league). Now he uses words. A soldier like me should not attempt to engage.

---

1   See *The Giftie*, Datura Press, for her story.

I saw you on the news, Points West, saving that girl. You are 'Mr Dulux' aren't you? He gave that stupid laugh again. Then ordered coffee from the waitress, who looked at me with concern. I think she might have had a thimble of Faery blood in her, and sensed the ancient combat that was about to take place. I gave her a reassuring smile.

I think you're ex-military. I recognised your gait, Michael. Did you think you were still walking through a minefield? Do you still hear the explosions and the screams when the PTSD kicks in? Is that why you spend all your time in cafés and tea shoppes? Because nothing bad can happen, and only good, harmless people come into them – unlike the pubs?

I might have frowned – what was he talking about? But he would have taken even such a mild facial tic as my parry to his thrust. In swordsmanship a true parry is a defensive action. Simple. It should be just wide enough to allow the attacker's blade to miss. Additional motion is wasteful. My silence was my parry. His thrust was pitiful, the line of advance all wrong.

The waitress came back with his coffee. Her hand was trembling slightly when she put his cup down and she kept looking at me. A large fly landed on the white Egyptian cotton tablecloth and came toward my crumbs. Flies cannot see in front. You can flick them to death by approaching them this way. Slowly. I did so.

Ne vous inquiétez pas, I said to the girl.

Sir Bruce frowned. He seemed surprised that I should have spoken in French.

He means Don't worry, said this self-styled McHaffee to her with a mad smile. She hurried away from him. *I think you might have frightened her* he stage-whispered.

Go, I told him. Simply, with power. It rippled across the room, the faux-crystal in the chandeliers tinkled. And then he asked the thing, most absurd:

The doctors I spoke to felt that you had all the signs of a recovering alcoholic. Tell me honestly… are you still 'dry'?

I closed my eyes and sank my chin to my chest. I shook my head. Not in answer to his question but through astonishment. Can humans be so completely stupid? How can du Lac, born of the great and ancient Lake, ever be 'dry'?!

It is said that those of the wild Faery race have neither compassion nor humour. But I tell you this: I raised my head to the white and ornate ceilings and roared with laughter. I was still laughing when they asked me to leave and escorted me outside.

Sir Bruce was like that fly. Une mouche. He appeared again in front of me, dirty, noisy, flitting around as I strode through the revolving doors of the Pump Rooms, out and across the Abbey churchyard. He knew better than to try and stop me. In ages gone I had unhorsed him in direct jousts many times. Sometimes in disguise. When he realised he could never become the Best Knight in the World, I think he decided to use his cruelty and become the worst. I say to all of his victims: Sorry.

Michael, Michael he hissed, using the stupid name he persisted with. *I just thought. You called me Sir Bruce sans Pitié. Are you into the whole King Arthur thing?*

I strode past him toward the Union Passage, a narrow alleyway of shops, packed with Japanese tourists and the sort of young beggars that used to crowd the outer gates of Camelot in times of famine.

Michael, if I am this character Sir Bruce, who are you? he called from behind me.

Two young heavily-armoured policemen approached me. No doubt I was about to be blamed for the damage actually done by my foe. Plus ca change…

No! came the voice of the madman from behind. *Leave him be. I'm Dr Eric McHaffee and he's a patient of mine! No violence, please, PLEASE!*

I laughed. There was no danger. I would never dream of hurting any policeman. They are there to serve the land and its monarch. Like me. I grabbed a newspaper – I think it was the *Bath Chronicle* – from a golden-hued tourist and rolled it into a tube. The two policemen withdrew their sad little expanding metal batons, flicked them into full length and approached me slowly. The narrowness of the Union Passage was in my favour. I dipped, I feinted, I twirled and turned. Voila! Two fierce jabs of my simple little weapon and they were down. The Japanese tourists took photographs. The beggars – known locally as crusties – roared their approval: *Pigs pigs pigs pigs pigs!* they chanted… though I cannot say why. Perhaps it is the local totem animal.

I felt sorry for my victims, they were only doing their duty. I frowned at the rough ones in the crowd. Put my finger to my lips. They went silent.

One of the policemen got out his pepper spray but – with my incredible speed – I ducked below its stream.

Sorry, I said to the poor, sweet Japanese girl who got the full blast. Then his partner fired his taser at me but I pulled his compatriot between us as a shield and the wicked little points sank harmlessly into the wretch's armour.

Forgive them, I said to the crowd, which was now watching with awe. Perhaps they thought it street theatre, like the Morris Men and buskers. Perhaps they merely enjoyed seeing a true Master of War at work. Most of the poor people in Bath seemed to have gathered there.

More police approached, but hampered by the watchers.

Go that way said a young man with unpleasing piercings in his eyebrows, lips, nose and ears, and the dank smell of earth about him. *We'll block the pigs' path.*

I did. And they did.

A crusty young man with a lean black dog on a string asked: *Who are you?*

I am the great du Lac, I said, as I disappeared into the crowd.

It's him! – It's him! – It's him! came a whisper from the malcontents of this kingdom, rippling outwards like a stream.

Of course! I heard Sir Bruce shout after me as the 'doctor' gave succour to the bewildered young policemen. *I get it now!*

Never.

Jamais.

Today is Thursday. Jeudi. Perhaps. For one of the Faery kind like myself the days run by like seconds in the minds of humans. It is Thursday and it is raining. Again. The sun has gone down and I am comfortable. I stay in my small *apartement* or 'flat' as the English so crassly term it and read. A knight like myself must keep in touch with the world and the peoples I have sworn to serve. If I look out of my front windows I see the tops of the buildings opposite catch the last light of the day, turning pink, then gold, then fading into shadows. From the window above the sink in my little kitchen I have a view of tree tops in the Royal Victoria Park. They move like waves, and make the calm sound of the sea.

My apartement is entirely white. The walls, curtains, doors, ceilings and even the floorboards. I distrust carpet. In combat it can slip. The furniture too, is white. There are no clocks, no mirrors. The white bookcases are filled with books in English and French.

I will explain: I, du Lac, do not belong to that political entity which now bears the name of 'France'. Nor to the one *they* call Angleterre, though I have lived here, because of my oath to Arthur, most of my long existence. In the days of my youth, in the great depths of the Time before Time, they were one land. Then came the Great Tremor which helped create La Manche, or the English Channel, which quickly filled with conger, like dead souls.

My nationality exists beyond mere geography and modern politics. Even so, I have great fondness for the tone and subtlety of all things 'French', and choose it to express myself. In England I am always on a Quest; when I am in France, I am home. Somehow. I have fought for both countries as a nameless – and always unknown – warrior.

As a creature of the Lake – and I will explain all in due course – I need good thick rock and earth around me, to hold the waters. I can use lakes as humans use doors. That is how I travel. I cannot go into the sea – the great bitter sea – because I would lose myself.

I do not know how I came to this apartement, My kind have 'absences'. Our lives are so long that we must have moments when we forget – or so the fat Merlin tells me. Though he himself is neither Human nor Faery so I do not entirely trust him.[2] And so – voilà – the Patterns are repeated from Age to Age. It is not reincarnation, mais non. Rejuvenation? Continuation? Perhaps.

I will tell you secrets about The Merlin later, but he told me a tale. Yesterday. A fable to help me understand. There was an ill-made man dressed in rags, he said, who walked into a store in Bath, known as Jollys. He walked, bent and troubled, in through the east door. He chose white clothes of best quality: underwear, socks, shirt, shoes and suit… white white white samite. He changed into them in a little

---

2   See *The Fat Git*, Skylight Press, for his story.

cubicle and when he emerged he was new. He shone. The people in the store watched in awe as he left by the west door.

So here I am in my pure cell on the top floor of an old house in Bath. The doorbell rings. Actually, it mutters. I have put tissue between the little hammer and the bell itself. There is no need for anyone to visit – except for Gwenevere of course. I have no name on the button of mine at the main entrance, though others do. Macleod, Coutts, Sally Hart – I forget the rest.

I know who the mutterer is. *Ring-ring!* The two syllables of young Kelvin. They are faster than usual. Frantic. *Ring-ring!* He is anxious. He is always anxious about something. It is a good trait to have as a Squire. Then, after the time it takes for a human to climb the 93 steep steps to my room, I hear the knock on my door. Unnecessary. He has a key. Where he gets the keys from I do not know. Yet resourcefulness and cunning are important skills in a Squire. I say nothing.

Are you all right? he asks. These are his first words to me every time. I have no idea what School of Chivalry he was attached to before he came to me, but they are fitting. Once I have finished his training and he has won his sword and spurs, I will sit down with him and we will talk as equals in rank – though never in experience or lineage.

He opens my door. Slowly.

Christ! he exclaims. He is panting from the climb.

Entrez I call over my shoulder, sarcastically, for he has done so already.

Kelvin appeared a week ago. I think. Perhaps more. He described himself as my Special Person, who will act as my keyworker. I blinked. I have fought my way out of locked cells and through iron bars to get to my Lady Gwenevere. I have no need for anyone to work keys. He showed me too, certain documents. He held them before me like shields. He called them Person Centred Plans, which were supported by Risk Assessments and Incident Reports. His lips moved but I never heard his words when he tried to explain. I dived into a submarine world before his very eyes, though he never realised. The water filled my ears and made me deaf to his nonsense.

So he is here again, a thin young man. A maiden. His clothes are too tight. Black jeans and boots, white shirt without collar whose sleeves are rolled up. His lank hair is fastened back in a pony-tail by an elastic band. He has an excess of nasal hairs protuding from his sharp nose like a thicket and I will tell him so.

Christ he says again, though more softly when he gets his breath back and looks around. *You've been busy.* He touches the surfaces, carefully, with the tip of one little finger. Very dainty. I tell him:

They are all dry – sec.

He sniffs the finger. An unpleasant gesture.

I like your suit.

My armour I say, though no more than that. I was long known as the mysterious White Knight. I was armoured thus when Gwenevere fell in love with me. I am sentimental. I defended her and the King a million times as an Unknown Warrior who never sought recognition. I kept my name from them as long as I could. That gave me power. When I first opened my visor to her and showed her my very handsome face, she was already in love.

He looks at my game of chess. The board is set cleverly on a little round table with a silver rim. It revolves. I can play against myself with a single turn of the board. This was Gwenevere's favourite game. We never seemed to finish one. She always found some excuse to disappear, after leaving me with a new challenge. Charming! When I play alone, the pieces move themselves in reply. It is Gwenevere doing that. It helps us maintain contact. She is trapped somewhere. I am always rescuing her. I think she sends me messages from the moves the pieces make. Alas, I am not erudite.

There are no Kings on the board he says.

I play by different rules.

He shakes his head and walks around, quizzically. He looks at my books.

Are you learning French?

How English. How very droll. I am silent.

You really are this Dulux guy, yah?

I am silent again. I allow him to absorb the atmosphere of my castle, my enchanted place. He is bewildered. He needs to learn.

Think, Kelvin... what does the word Dulux mean?

It's a paint. A brand name. By the looks of it, you've used gallons of the stuff here, yah?

Think Kelvin. Be clever. Dulux. Du. Lux. Or even, perhaps, du Lux. Of the light. Je l'ai dit.

Pardon? I don't speak French.

You are pardoned. For now. Du Lux. Of the Light. I said it.

Oh, ha ha hardi hah he chuckles. His lips seal up like an anus as he does so.

Kelvin, if you are to be my Squire, you will learn to speak with elegance.

To be your what?

Squire. You will learn to avoid those dreadful little apostrophes which – what is your term? – elide two words.

What?

Pour example: 'I'll'. You must learn to use 'I will'.

Why, for God's sake?

*When God spoke to Moses on the mountain did He say: 'I'm that I'm'? Did Martin Luther King say 'I've a dream'? They are, and always must be: 'I **am** that I **am**' and also 'I **have** a dream' Said thus, they changed the world of Humankind.*

He sits back on the white wooden chair and leans his elbow on my white kitchen table. His skin is white, pale white against my white walls, he could almost be a Faery himself. I wonder if he has ever known love – true love – the sort that a man would die for. There is a faint flicker of amusement at the corner of his thin lips.

That's why Dr McHaffee called you Michael. As you didn't give us any name, and came out with all sorts of guff, he felt you were taking the Mickey. Hence Michael. You're doing it now.

Zut! I say. I know he will learn.

Now, your homework – votre devoirs – is to find three examples in which the nasty apostrophe reduces your magnificent viral language to absurdity.

Michael, that is not in my contract.

No. But it is in mine. It will fit you to meet and serve the highest in the land.

Yah? So who?

Squire, I say softly, in confidential tones, *I have held Queens in my arms.*

He laughs. He gives a very coquettish look.

So have I, dearie.

That is good. I like a Squire with wit. If they also have the English Disease (and many do) I do not worry.

And if I do this? If I 'improve' my speech.

Then I will teach you to fight.

That's defo not in my contract, you couldn't –

He has to stop. I move with lightning speed and throw him on the white floorboards, but cradling the back of his head and taking his body weight so there is no pain. Beneath the hair, his skull is very small, like a baby's. He trembles like one.

I'm scared. I'm really scared of you he whispers. *Please don't do this…*

His pupils are wide with terror. I can see myself reflected in them. I am Who I am. It feels good.

Squire… you are now the safest man in England. First, I will never harm you. I give you my oath. Second, I will never let another harm you. All the Bad People in the world could try to attack you now but they will fail. None will get past me. Comprenez?

Yes, oui – whatever. Please will you let me up?

I let him see deep into my own eyes. His widen even more. I release him from my simple grip and he stands up, smoothes the wrinkles from his absurd clothes. He notices that with a single snap I have removed the elastic from that stupid pony tail. Nervously, he spreads his hair wide on his shoulders, unable to speak.

You are wearing eye-liner I say.

Only a little.

Then stop that. Today.

He is breathing heavily. It is not fear.

When you have done your homework I will teach you how to fight. I will not touch you. I will not expect you to use or carry weapons. Yet I will make you invincible.

Whatever.

And now, tidy this little apartement before you go.

That's not in my –

I raise one powerful eyebrow. I have stood alone on bridges and stopped platoons of soldiers with this eyebrow.

Okay. Okay.

And then, et puis, you will call me 'Sir' until you win your spurs. Or until the 'contract' becomes void. My contract, not yours.

Okay. Sir. So… so where's – I mean where is – the hoover?

This evening, Friday, I was sitting outside the little eating place – it could hardly be called a restaurant – on Bath Spa railway station, on the eastbound platform. I delight in the very name: Bath Spa. For du Lac, the words themselves have healing. Tears, you see, as my foster mother told me, come directly from the heart. She called them – and still calls them – the 'water of the heart'. I, the warrior who has shed lakes of tears for his woman, could submerge himself in a place like this.

I had a large mug of café au lait, a croissant that was not at all French, and was enjoying the moment. I like such places. People are going, or coming. They are in-between worlds. Changing, moving, like time itself – perhaps. Although we are far from the sea the reddening sky is full of gulls which swim like fish on the currents that surge and stay between the seven green hills of the little city.

It was Vespers. I heard the great bells of the Abbey chime six times, rippling the air. Church bells tolling remind me of Old Things. They can pin me to the spot. I was – what is the word – reminiscing? I can remember minute details from centuries ago, yet am hazy about yesterday. It is Gwenevere who holds everything together, like the silver thread in a necklace of gold amulets.

The great trains thundering past me were so like the huge armoured knights that I had fought so often at the jousting. Knights like: Sir Yvain, Kay the seneschal, Sagramour the Impetuous, Galegantin, Dodinel the Wild, Gales the Bald and Aguissant of Scotland. Countless others. With their visors down they were faceless metal silver creatures that hurtled toward me in straight lines, roaring.

Because I was often anonymous (or they would not have fought me) I adopted different styles. I would slump in the saddle like an old man; I would hold my lance as if were too heavy; I would sway from side to side as if drunk; or ride as if afraid. But then – et puis – at the final moment I would strike, at the greatest speed, with perfect symmetry. They would fall. Always.

Sometimes, if they were very old or very young and needed either tolerance or encouragement, I would simply use my shield to deflect their own lances, making no attempt to strike with my own. They would thunder past, unharmed, but with lessons learned.

I was thinking of those days when I felt a large but gentle hand on my shoulder. Stubby fingers. The nails had been bitten to the quick, no half-moons.

Sir... come back from the platform's edge. You're standing too close. You might get sucked in.

The man's face was familiar. Clean shaven, like a soldier before parade. Short black hair and pale blue eyes. It was wary but not hostile. Respectful and puzzled. He said something but the express train roared past us and took his words away. I was not engaged by his conversation because I was drawn to the nun on the platform opposite. The platform which takes people into the West.

I admire and try to protect those who have taken Oaths and thus wrestle with demons. Always. Loyalty can matter more than cause. This nun belonged, I was certain, to the Order of St. Clare. One of the Poor Clares, as they are called – not always respectfully these days. I felt that she was not there by chance: that thin woman in the dark habit looking to the east for her train: that dark shadow with the white strip on her brow containing her brightest hopes for humankind. Leaning slightly to one side, as if she carried a burden. Nothing in my life is by chance. Gwenevere spent some time hiding as a nun in Amesbury. Perhaps this one had a message? I saw her go into the waiting room. The automatic door opened for her and closed immediately, with a loud crack.

There are railings between the platform opposite and its car park. Beyond them a dozen crusties were assembled, watching me keenly, Many of them seemed to have rough hounds, on rough leads. When the creatures became aware of my gaze they sat down as a pack and watched, tongues lolling and panting. I do not like dogs yet they knew the pack leader. Me.

*Sir…*the man persisted. *Don't worry. I'm not on duty now. I was told you needed help.*

I frowned.

I'm one of the two policemen that tried to apprehend you in Union Passage. Don't worry, you're not in trouble.

I was worried. Not by him. But by the drunken mob of Welshmen, rugby fans, which poured into the room after the nun.

Listen… I can't explain this. But… I nearly won a bronze medal in the world championships for Judo. Yet you threw me around like a toy. And I had the mad feeling that when my mate panicked and fired the taser, you lifted me so the points would hit my body armour and not my face.

Bien sûr. I am very strong. Very fast. I think I can slow down time, also.

I must go, I told him.

There is a tunnel which connects the two platforms but I jumped down and ran across the tracks, just avoiding the London train, amid screams. It was like being at the tourney again, with the crowd going wild behind the barriers and the nobles eating lamprey at their feasts and the starving folk below them grasping at their crumbs.

The door opened before me, but not fast enough for my liking. I think I broke the mechanism when I pushed.

The nun sat in the corner, her thin shoulders squeezing into the angles of the room for protection. There were old photographs of the Great Western Railway on the walls, a false fireplace, and metal chairs that looked as if they had been made from bits of unwanted armour. Full of holes. She had a little book on her lap as if it might protect her. It was old, with a dark blue cover, flecked with age. I assumed it was the New Testament, and she was taking comfort from the Apocalypse. The boyos were all around, like wasps, their loud Welsh insults buzzing against her. To them, it was a great joke that she could not understand their comments and suggestions.

I squeezed between them – gently – and hunched around so that my broad shoulders would take the impact and venom of their stings. The tormentors assumed from my mien that I was part of their game. Their suggestions as to where I should put my lance were obvious yet still disgusting.

Sister Clare I said, and she looked at me sharply. Her eyes took on a brief almost golden sheen. Sometimes a nun is more than a nun, just as a woman is always more than a woman. *You know that you will come to no physical harm when I am here. I can also stop their vulgarity.*

Because I whispered, the increasingly tedious boyos thought I was also making obscene comments. Their noise rose another level.

Do you know Who I am, Sister?

She looked at me hard. The brief golden sheen again, no longer than a blink.

I think you are probably a child of the devil but sent by God to do His work.

I have sometimes thought that. How do you want me to proceed?

No blood, please.

Of course not! I knew a Pope who went into battle with a mace. He would kill without a qualm as long as he drew no blood.

They called that malecide, she said with pursed lips, flicking away a hand which sought to remove her wimple. *They could kill people if they thought it would defend their Lamb.*

I was surprised by her tone, and they way she said 'They', as if she was not entirely a part of their system.

Can you stop them without killing them or breaking blood? If I was younger I would kick the shit out of them.

I warmed to her.

Sister Clare… see the way I press my finger on my own thigh? I will use no more strength than this.

She nodded. I stood up and escorted her through the broken door, shielding her from the drunken louts and their rugby songs.

Take her I said to the off-duty policeman who had followed me the long way around, and who had been watching all this through the dirty windows. I know he hoped to learn something, and get a medal in future.

The mob tried to surge after us: their train was arriving. I pushed them back. I did the next things in slow sequence so that my watcher might learn.

Number 1. With my index finger I pushed – no more than that – into his solar plexus at a slight upward angle. He gasped for air. We were close up. My approach looked affectionate. The others did not see what I had done. They thought I was trying to kiss him.

Number 2. Simple. I turned him with an affectionate smile and jabbed his right kidney with my thumb. The beauty of this is that the pain is not felt immediately, but grows and makes the victim give off a kind of whale-song of agony seconds later.

Number 3. I simply kicked back with the edge of my heel into a certain spot on his knee-cap. Again, with the right angle – and I always achieve this – it will paralyse the whole leg.

Number 4. I gave that one an insane grin, pushed him gently into the same corner they had trapped the nun and told him gently, in Welsh, that I, the great du Lac, would rip out his heart and send it to his Mam. He shat himself.

I saw the man at the window watching all this. To him, I must have looked like a pickpocket moving gracefully through a crowd, at close quarters, almost gently. I nodded to him and winked. Courtesy costs nothing, even during extreme violence.

Outside the monstrous train had arrived. A recorded voice was saying Please Mind the Gap.

The nun looked at me with the slightest of smiles on her pale cold face.

Now do you know who I am, Sister Clare?

Most definitely a devil. Still possibly sent by God.

I have been called worse.

People were pouring off the train, we stood aside for them. I saw that her book was not a Bible at all, and that the cover was the colour of the night sky, and the staining was a clear image of the Milky Way.

The Little Book of the Great Enchantment! I said in wonder, for this was a Faery book, long since lost to both worlds. *You are no nun, you are –*

This is for you, she said, opening it.

My heart sang. Inside was the greatest story of my long life. It was told not in human words, for the pages were blank, but in the single forget-me-not that had been pressed at the centre.

I took it from her. She stepped into the carriage and looked at me through the open window of the door, as the great machine started to thunder into the West.

Du Lac, she called above the increasing noise of engine and metal wheels. *You have won through to Gorre at last. Now you must find her and win through to peace.*

The four wasps that I had swatted staggered out of the waiting room.

Call the police croaked the Number 1 to my watcher. *We'll do the bastard. You was a witness.*

I am the police, sonny. Nah, never saw a thing...

The crusties were chanting behind me: *Du Lux Du Lux Du Lux!*

Of the Light. I wish I had shadows.

Forget-me-Nots...I will tell you about these. They grow in bogs and wet places and beside streams and rivers. How can du Lac not love such a perfect little flower, with its five petals the colour of a blue moon and a warm sun at the very centre? Gwenevere told me she fell in love with me because of a forget-me-not. I was still the Unknown Knight who had just defeated in a tourney: Yvain of the White Hands,

Yvain the Crooked, Caradoc Shortarm, the Gay Galantin (twice), plus Caradigas, Agloas, Magloas and – if I remember rightly – the King of Marés.

The sky was a fathomless bowl above the world, a deep, deep blue such as I had only seen before in Lake Nemi, where my foster-mother would often take me as a boy. And I was, that afternoon and beneath that sky, magnifique. Irresistible. Fearless. Yet when I approached her for my prize, I trembled. She knew me as nothing more than a suit of noisy metal. I saw the most beautiful woman who ever lived. Pale. Pale as the Moon, with the white blood of a Faery Queen. Long hair which could be blonde, or could be silver, changing as she turned, changing with her mood. It poured from her head onto her shoulders and lower. Soft. Soft as light itself. Green eyes, very rich in colour. Thin red lips that seemed to threaten a smile. She was also shapely, slim, with – I will not say more. That is private. She was perfect. Not for Arser but, oh certainement, for me.

She waved me over to where she sat with her ladies. Arser was not there that day, he was away in Galles, killing Welshmen and perhaps avoiding his wife.

I clunked over. I had taken a pounding from Caradoc Shortarm and the cuisse and greaves which protected my legs had been battered solid and would not flex. I walked stiff-legged. I felt that everyone was laughing at me, despite my deeds.

I could not kneel so I stood before her, head bowed, almost in prayer. I had not even lifted my visor. The huge crowd was hushed. I could feel them lapping toward me, desperate to know who this powerful knight was, and what his secret might be. The only mark I had was my round white shield with bend gules. It was hot as Hades in the armour, after all the fighting under the endless sun, yet I shook as if with cold.

You are a strong and fearless knight Gwenevere said, and her voice was like a cool stream which rippled over me. *I think I should fear you.*

I had lost my tongue. I think she sensed this because she leaned forward and lifted my visor, and made me look into her eyes. I gasped. It was as if a long, lost part of me had just been found. As if broken things within me had suddenly been mended. I straightened up and trembled.

What is your name?

I was shy. As I had only recently learned it myself and hardly trusted my name's truth, or even its sound, I did not like to say.

You are shy! she teased, delighted, seeing right through the armour, right through to Me as no-one else has ever done since.

I will give you this, bold sir knight, if you tell your name.

This, was a small bunch of forget-me-nots.

My name is, I have been told, Lancelot du Lac. Of the Lake. Son of King Ban of Benwick, in Brittany, and Queen Elen. I am a King's son.

As the words forced themselves through my awkwardness I must have sounded pompous. She smiled. It was like a jewel thrown into a pond. Because she was Queen all the ladies in her retinue smiled, and the smiles spread outward through the other knights and their servants and beyond them through the whole crowd. Even the hounds, horses and asses seemed to be smiling at me. I stood in the centre of all this, scowling, as she handed me a small posy of forget-me-nots.

Have you ever held flowers wearing gauntlets which cover from the fingers to the forearms? Made of heavy metals with 92 hinges, twice that many joints and numberless rivets, each glove soaked in other people's blood?

I would never crush those flowers that she gave me, or break them. I used more skill, more strength, more concentration holding them in the palms of my iron hands than I had done in all the battles that day.

Look, my queen whispered to her lady-in-waiting, but loud enough for me to hear. *He's like a little boy!*

I shone. I am the most grizzled, battered, effective fighting man who has ever lived but I have always felt like a little lost boy inside. She saw. She saw Who I was, and am.

There is a legend about me from Germany. It is not true, but it captures a Truth. Once, the story goes, Gwenevere and I were walking along the banks of a river. I was holding a posy of the forget-me-nots she had just given me. The banks were muddy, slippery, I fell into the river and the weight of my armour pulled me down. As I was drowning I threw the posy to my beloved and shouted *Forget-me-not!* Since then, it was often worn by ladies as a sign of faithfulness and enduring love.

I, who do not smile often, smile ruefully at that last. It has always been du Lac who was faithful, with the enduring love that caused him to destroy kingdoms. She had her King, Arser, who spoiled everything. Despite everything that happened, I was never totally secure in her love for me.

It was The Merlin who noticed what passed between us. I think it troubled him. As though it might spoil his perpetual schemes and plans.

He tried to give me advice. He was eating a plateful of fried nightingales and larks tongues at the time. Greasy sleeves, from wiping his lips. This is the man, remember, who had made a fool of himself with that little fée cocotte, Vivienne. The one with blonde spiky hair and pointed bosoms that some people mistook for Nimué. Who trapped him in a cave and stole all his secrets.

He said: *You cannot love someone without fearing them*

Nonsense I snapped, though I knew every word was true. There was not a man or wild beast on this world that would cause me anguish, but I feared Gwenevere. Feared her in the sense that I never wanted to lose her. Never wanted to do or say anything foolish which might cause this. Sought never to perform an ungallant act or utter a thoughtless comment. It almost paralysed me in the early days of what became our courtship. It was not so much that I was a hesitant man inside a suit of armour; truly, du Lac in those days was more like a heavy suit of armour which happened to have a nervous creature inside.

If it had not been for the fact that I was so infernally handsome and that something passed between us, through our eyes and into our souls at our first meeting, I think she might have tilted her charms toward Gawaine instead. Even if she was his aunt by marriage.

Yet I feel that my time is ending. There are things I must tell you. I will speak of Arser when I first met him. When I called him Arthur. My king. I will – for this Human moment – call this man Arthur because it is a different soul to the one I later knew. Or else it was I, du Lac, who became different. Perhaps.

When Arthur was young he was a great bear. He stood on his hind legs roaring among the heavens and through the worlds. His call made nape hairs prickle and the bloods of Humans and some Fées sing. People were drawn to him – Good People. It was not his fighting ability but what he fought for – a stable land. Harmony. Justice tempered with kindness. But justice first. I who have served many kings and queens have observed through the centuries that firm justice, consistently applied, breeds less discontent in a kingdom than soft mercy, randomly administered.

As a Warrior he was majestic. Fearless. When I arrived those glory days were over so I, du Lac, became his champion.

But understand this: Arthur was Merlin's creation. His toy, almost. He brought Humans and Fées together and ensured a royal mating. How much of this was through magick, or lies, I do not know. When Arthur was born Merlin stole him, as the Lady of the Lake stole me. He ensured the boy – the wonderchild – was brought up in the Forest Sauvage, not knowing who he was – again, like me. He was a Green Man, his destiny being that he should never quite die, and always be ready to come to the country's aid when it was threatened. Like me, he had a magick sword: his called Excalibur, mine Seure. We could have been twins.

It was in the Great Hall at Camelot when I first met him. Sun was coming through the narrow slits of their tall windows. Pennons of red and yellow and green were rippling in the drafts, making their images of lions, boars, wyverns, white horses and griffins seem alive. Bursts of colour and motion against the still grey stone and smoked wood of the room. The floor was covered in fresh straw, each stalk cut to an exact length. I walked on gold.

Arthur was… magnificent. Long blond hair and green eyes. He faced me as though he had expected me. I hoped that he would not be disappointed. He was not! When I looked into those eyes I glimpsed deep forests of an ancient world, through which strode the ghosts of Sacred Kings like the beads on a necklace. Although he was little more than medium height, he towered over everyone, and wore the title of the Pendragon like a cloak of stars.

He spoke. His voice was deep, it came from around his heart. Lower. A lilting accent. Scottish? No. He was how every man would sound and look if they could but choose.

He seduced us all. Man and woman, Human and Fée. I took an oath to protect the land and the people, high and low, rich or poor. To defend it against all foes, forever, including the increasingly troublesome Saracens. Truly, vraiment, I would have sworn any oath that he demanded. As I turned and walked away I saw the amusement on the faces of the whole court. They had all been bewitched by him. They understood. Approved.

Knights of the Table Round? They were Fools for Love, no more, no less.

That was the True Arthur. That one died. Or the Arthur in my heart did. What was left became Arser to me from then on.

I am still angry.

I rose at Matins, as always, which is what Humans call 6 a.m., drank strong coffee and sat quietly in my armchair. It was cold. Raining. I sat in my chair and watched the clouds swimming past the chimneys of the high buildings opposite, like spawning salmon. There had been alarums in the night and much disturbance. These things were not my responsibility, so I had slept deeply. Despite this I felt weary. As if I had been wearing my armour for weeks. Years.

After what seemed like a mere blink I heard the church bells tolling for the Third Hour, of Terce. I knew it must be Sunday. Certainement. These things anchor me else I would float away.

There was tap on the door and I knew it was Sir Bruce. I did not turn to greet or acknowledge or even scorn. He has developed other ways of stabbing me in the back over the centuries.

Sorry I haven't been to see you earlier. I've had a few issues with another resident, as I expect you heard.

Silence from me, deep silence. I am a deep-rooted frond at the bottom of a lake, swaying gently in the currents. With my extraordinary vision I could follow every step and gesture and facial expression as he wandered around my magical little cell.

My my you've certainly been busy. Kelvin said. I thought he was exaggerating. And you've been raiding the Oxfam Bookshop in town. I mean literally.

Silence, always silence. This tactic can cause opponents like Sir Bruce to lower their guard. He took a white kitchen chair, spun it around on one leg and sat facing me, with his arms around the chair's back. Disrespectful. Jejune.

Michael… I have to call you that until you tell me – or anyone – otherwise. I don't know what to make of you. Shall I tell you what we do know?

I stared beyond him, over his head and out of my windows, toward a land and a Time before Times. My nose wrinkled slightly from his pungent aftershave. He had the air of a man who had just had sex. Poor sex.

The police first saw you, late at night, stark bullock naked, trying to cross the swollen River Avon by walking along the edge of Pulteney Weir.

It was hardly that. It was a Sword Bridge, as the fat Merlin can confirm. I will tell more later.

You could have drowned.

I, du Lac, am always drowning. It is the way I live.

When they got you safely across and into the Parade Gardens they wrapped you in their silver thermal blankets and asked you who you were, and where you thought you were, your only comment was GAW.

Actuallement it was Gorre. This is the place where Gwenevere is kept prisoner. It is the place where every man must try to enter if they are to find a pure love, which they must bring out from the Wasteland of their lives. Few ever get there. Few ever try.

And your only possession was the silver ring you are wearing now.

Which bears inside the words Love begets Love, and was given to me by Nimué to help guide me through the Human world and protect me from enchantments. Even now I do not fully understand this terrible message.

You lost consciousness and spent three days in the Royal United Hospital where you became an object of huge amazement because of your scarred body. Specialists came from all over to marvel.

I had no knowledge of this. I hid my embarrassment. The thought of strange people staring at my naked body is troubling. Sir Bruce took a small notebook out of his inner pocket and started to list my scars.

They counted 9 obvious bullet wounds – all healed of course – but of three different calibres.

Monte Cassino, Gold Beach in Normandy, and that dreadful battle for Caen.

Large areas of your skin show scarring consistent with chlorine gas!

Hill 60, near Ypres. That day in the Great War when chivalry in battle finally died. The British Army was right to reply in kind.

Two indentations – and don't ask me how they determined this – which looked as if they had been caused by musket balls, for god's sake!

God had nothing to do with it. They were probably from my days with Wellington during his Indian campaign. Perhaps. You must know that because of my oath to Arser I have always fought for Britain – though never against France.

Then your forearms, shoulders and legs showed evidence of long and very old cuts that could only have been done by large knives.

Swords. Idiot! They could have been done in any century. The fighting man lost something when guns superseded cold steel.

Your rib-cage showed apparent signs of having been smashed by heavy objects.

Ah. Senlac Hill, where I fought to protect the divine Harold Godwinson against the Normans – who were definitely NOT French.

Oh – and also two and possibly three places where your body seemed to have been pierced by what they could best describe as poles or rods.

Lances. Wielded by the King of a Hundred Knights, when I was defending Arser's honour. Not that he had much left by that time.

And most bizarre of all, you've got a bar-code tattooed in your inner arm. What's that about?

Bar-code? No, scratch marks caused by the monster that I helped Arser drag from the lake on Cader Idris. What did Sir Kay call it? Ah oui, an Addanc.

Despite all possible efforts no-one knows who you are. Nor will you communicate properly with Kelvin your keyworker here in Tigh Aisling. You know what Tigh Aisling is, don't you? It's a place that I created to stop you being sent to another place. In crude and old and brutal terms I'm trying to keep you out of the asylum. Tigh Aisling means –

House of Dreams, I told him. I know the Gaelic.

His thrust had struck me a light blow. He looked delighted by my response. I was annoyed with myself.

To be honest, in my professional role and with many years of dealing with people like yourself, I don't know whether I should ride along with you for a little while and try to steer you in a good direction. Or whether I should come right at you and try to unseat you from these Arthurian fantasies. You told one of the crusties in the Union Passage that you were du Lac. And you call me Sir Bruce sans Pitié – which I quite like, actually. Please, tell me who you really are?

The man was absurd. Insane. Behind him, out of his sight, a piece was being moved on my chess board by an invisible hand.

Look, we feel you are ex-Army, though the authorities deny it. I wonder if you have been held prisoner, somewhere, and tortured. You've been trained only to give Name Rank and Serial Number but you won't give even this much to us, who are trying to help you.

Another piece was being moved. Gwenevere was being insistent. I would have to get rid of this Doctor without Medicine, as they once called such fools, so that I could fathom her message.

Despite all this the doctors described you as being in amazing nick, as one specialist termed it. He had served in the Falklands. Plus the nurses all adored you.

I will joust with you tomorrow, I said to get rid of him.

By that I understand that you will talk with me. Okay okay... tomorrow it is. Until then –

Go! I said with power, and he went. As an afterthought, he turned the chair back the way it had been. He also glanced at the chess pieces, as if he noticed that two of them had been moved.

Oh – one last thing. When you were unconscious in the hospital, a woman came and sat by the bed all night. She said she was your wife. Then she disappeared before anyone could get any details.

Go... I said more softly this time. It was not Gwenevere. It was a woman who has fished for my affections all my life and chased me through madness.

I du Lac have secrets. I will tell you the first one.

I am of mixed race.

As a few people still remember (but not many), in the Times before Time there were two races on Earth and gates between the worlds. Sometimes Humans can step through, even today. More often it is the fées who step into the Human realm. My Gwenevere could move easily from one world to another. I, du Lac, have no such easy skill. I suppose I blame my Human father for that.

It is a heavy burden to me, being mixed race. My armour? I wear it without effort. Yet being both Human and Faery is the cause of all my weighty problems.

I have a little book that I took from the charity shop. I did not see why I should pay, because it was about me. It was a book I have read many times over a thousand years, in several languages. It is called, simply, Lancelot of the Lake. The stories about me are badly written, without style or grace, largely nonsense. When I read them I feel as modern 'celebrities' must feel when they see their deeds and misdeeds in the newspapers. Exasperation. Anger. Also, amusement.

The anonymous writer of this livre almost got it right when he noted: 'He had a beautiful complexion, not too white or brown, but a mixture of the two; you might call it light brown.'

The dark skin comes because I am part Human and Faery. My father was King Ban of Benwick. He was one of the few male fées to find a way through. My mother was the very mortal princess Elen. They lived in what is now known as Brittany. My mother – my birth-mother – became known as the Queen of Great Sorrows when I was taken from her as a child. She walked her Human world clad in black, her face so far into her cowl that none saw her features, all the rest of her days. I am told that she had the sort of understanding that only deep suffering can bring. Her servants adored her. Evidement. She spent years staring into the depths of puddles, ponds, streams, rivers, lakes and indeed her own depths, calling me by my true name: Galahad.

No, no I am not that same little prig, my supposed son, who chased after that pudding basin known as the Holy Grail. Galahad was *my* true name, my birth name and first name, though it was never used by anyone save my mother. Perhaps.

I do not know where 'Lancelot' came from. What does it mean? Is it from the French? Lancer l'eau? To throw water? The fat Merlin teased me that it may have been an English term: Lance Lot. A lot of lance. Or Big Dick perhaps? he suggested, with his tongue stuck boldly in his stupid cheeks. Then again, much later, he told me another meaning, perhaps a true meaning, which shook me badly. I will tell you about such things later. Soon.

My foster mother, the Lady of the Lake, had three names for me: Handsome Foundling, King's Son and Rich Orphan – none of them the infernal Lancelot. These names were not said in words. They were concepts, thrown into my heart, that the Human side of me translated in a clumsy way. Clumsy they may be, but you can sense the respect that my foster mother felt for me, so perhaps I was loved by her after all. Or merely respected. Or feared.

But Lancelot... *bof!* Even Gwenevere in our most tender moments never called me that. I think, however, she decided that if she called no man by his first name then she would never discomfort herself by calling out the wrong one: Arthur! Lancelot! To her, I was always Sir Knight, said teasingly. And sometimes Monsieur Chevalier, when she tried to speak my native tongue. I do not know what she called Arthur. Because he became so pompous it was probably My Leige.

My fée father was murdered by the evil Claudas. They removed his head. Put it on a spear. And so we lost all our lands in a heartbeat. A moment later I was stolen by Nimué, the Lady of the Lake. I have to think the two events were connected, and no accident of timing.

The author of that little book recorded this. He described how Nimué approached my devastated mother and said: *Dear sweet friend... put the child down, for he will have hardship and sorrow enough from now on, now that he has lost all the land that should have been his.*

My mother put me on that land which I had just lost and Nimué grabbed me, went straight to the lake and jumped in 'with her feet together', as the writer noted. Mother might have jumped in too if the squire had not held her back.

In truth, I am not sure whether to blame my mother for her stupidity, or the squire for his presumption. I have had hardship and sorrow since then, certainement. The writer went on to describe how we – Nimué and I – lived with knights and damsels in the lake – 'which is in fact a magic illusion'.

Not so. There is a song inside the blood of the Faery kind. When they step into the Human world they lower the tones, suppress the high notes and take on flesh. I cannot explain it better. When they wish to return the song becomes high again, the sound of stars. It looks to Humans as if they are sinking down into a lake.

My own song as someone of mixed race is heavy, dark, filled with melancholy. If I could make my blood sing as Gwenevere's I might… I might…

I am not sure.

Kelvin, my Squire, is cleaning all the surfaces of my furniture with a strange feathery brush. He assures me it attracts and collects the dust, though I see no evidence of that. Still, he is cheerful. He sings as he works. I notice, approvingly, that his nose hairs have been trimmed but that his hair has been cut into a modern style which sweeps down over one eye. He will need to correct that.

I am studying the chessboard. Most of the pawns remain, two castles and one Bishop. There is only one knight but two Queens left on the board. I know who they are. There is a pattern in the way they are placed by hands other than mine. There is a message.

Kelvin finds a sheet of paper with lists of lakes. I have been to them all, when not on duty. He reads the names that I have ticked off one by one, starting at Lac de Guerlédan in Brittany, taking in nearby lakes at Jugon and Arguenon just in case, then every spa town in France from Aix-en-Provence to Vittel. Every spa town in England from Ashbourne to Woodhall Spa. The four Places of Waters in Wales, four in Scotland, plus Galway and Lisdoonvarna in Ireland. I arrived at the latter at a time when masses of women were in search of a husband, and had twenty-seven proposals of marriage before I fled.

He makes no connection between these possibilities and my ancient quest to find Gwenevere at the Place of Waters. Which might be here in Bath. I hope. I desperately hope.

With my extraordinary all around vision I notice that, when standing behind me, he folds the list and puts it in his pocket. It does not trouble me. His oaths were all toward Sir Bruce. There are times when a Squire can serve two masters. I will tell him, soon, that Sir Bruce lies. He always lies. He uses his lies to lead his victims down a certain forest trail. When he has ambushed and crushed them, he uses more lies to deny that trail ever existed. Kelvin may not believe me at first – few do – but he will. Meanwhile, I keep my

Little Book of Great Enchantments safely in my inside pocket, next to my heart and safe from theft. I can feel the forget-me-nots inside it, like arteries.

Dr. McHaffee is coming later, remember? he says with excitement in his voice.

I do not remember. Had I ever been told? I have no intention of meeting him yet, not until the field of combat is to my advantage. I need to find The Merlin first.

Sir… sir… he says.

Quoi? What? I say.

I have done my homework. And I have not elided any words for 48 hours.

There is a teasing air to his words. A not-unpleasing trait for a Squire. Yet I have to ask him: *What?* Living in the world of Humans, my memory is like the very tip of a wavelet on the surface of my lake. The real life is in the imperturbable depths.

Okay, okay, here is the first…

He babbles, but I do not listen. I feel something of import is on the way. A chill current which seeks to drag me into new depths.

Yah? he asks me, seeking approval for his nonsense.

Did I appoint him as Squire or Jester? In days long gone jesters were often used to take bad news to the King. Messengers were expendable – and usually were – but good jesters were hard to come by.

He seemed hurt that I did not respond to his absurdity, and his fractured versions of speeches by Churchill, Shakespeare and his renditions of songs by someone called Zeppelin. He creased with his own laughter at the words 'A whole lot of love' but it meant nothing to me. Rien.

Kelvin, stop your prattling. I must teach you how to fight. You might need to protect my back some day.

Sir, really, there is no need for that. In any case we would have to fill in so many Risk Assessments.

Hark! Can you hear those bells, Kelvin?

Bells? On a Monday morning?

Your 'Risk Assessments' sound the death knell of the courageous Englishman.

Ooh I know what you mean. Sir.

And those High Visibility jackets that everyone wears everywhere.

I don't wear one. Sir.

Stop being a creep and then I will teach you how to win any fight. Any.

His face lit up when I suggested this and then it fell.

Ha ha hardi hah… Look, sir, I'm – I mean, I am – not your alpha male. Probably not even beta or gamma or even delta male.

You were bullied at school.

I was.

You will never be bullied again. I give you my word.

He was curious.

You will not hurt me? Or throw me on the floor again?

Did I not give you my word?

Okay. Okay. Do I have to work out?

Pah. Take this stick, I said, offering him a short length of garden cane.

So, er what do I do? Poke them in the eye? he asked, disappointed. I felt sorry for him. He was clearly a young squire who has known much betrayal.

No, you must look at this stick and decide to break it. You must break it as quickly as if your life depended on it. Use all your strength in one sharp movement. With a loud HAH!

He jumps.

Can you do that?

He looks at the stick. Pulls it back and forth between his two hands. Gives a look as if he might make a rude joke but saw my intensity. He is not sure.

Kelvin, break that stick as if your life and that of your loved ones depended on it, as if you are avenging your father's murderer. Or punishing all those who ever scorned you and pushed your head down toilets.

He looks at the stick. I can see years of torture and torment imbued within its short length.

HAH! he cries. A goodly yell. Then hands me the broken bits with an expression that says *So?*

So… if you are attacked in such a way that you can grab it, then snap your enemy's little finger. They always try to protect their balls or face. They never protect the little fingers. You snap. Hard. Like that. No hesitation, no worrying that you might make him more angry and hurt you even more. Snap Snap Snap! Once the little finger is broken, the fight is over. No matter how big they are, or how drunk.

He feels his own little fingers in some wonder.

Have you broken many such in your time?

In my time! Oh such naiveté. In my time I have broken countless such bones. I never want a fight to escalate. I have compassion. It is kindness. The boy is pensive. I am enjoying being the master. He enjoys my mastery. I also know that he is trying to keep me occupied until Sir Bruce arrives.

Squire, every item in this little apartement can be used as a weapon. Some are obvious like the knives. Those thin kitchen knives that you used for my breakfast have what I call 'focal points'. Such as cameras have. Regardez... I hold this upward by the very tip, like so. Watch. I keep the flat of the blade toward the door. I throw as I might throw a dart. But – watch closely – just before I release I give a little flick of the wrist.

My kitchen knives are all like the old misericords: short black handles and long thin, silver blades which would strike through the gaps between armour plates and deliver the death stroke, which is also the mercy stroke. Hence the name. In fact I took a set from a shop in Bath called Kitchens where a beautiful young blonde woman, so like a faery herself, was quite happy to pass me a set, and ask for nothing – though I acted like a father or uncle and gave her some money for sweets, as fair exchange. I heft the blade in my hands. I am ambidextrous of course. Allow it to 'talk' to me, then throw it with a flourish.

Tra-La!

It quivers in the door. I do not know why the blade turns slightly in flight so that the blade hits the vertical grain of the wood. I do know that if I stood closer, or further away, it would not strike with the tip and the weapon would be wasted.

This larger knife... watch again.

I step back two paces. I throw with more vigour. It thuds next to the other. The two black handles against the white door look like speech marks. Kelvin is impressed. I am not sure if it is to do with my technique, or with my innate mastery of such black arts.

I couldn't – could not – use a knife. Sir.

Then look around.

Well, the pans are obvious.

Bon! There are few more joyous weapons than copper-bottomed pans. I killed two fallschirmjagers in Normandy with one, during house-to-house fighting.

Fall – whatty?

German paratroopers. Bad people.

I seemed to strike a chord.

*Have you met Miss Macleod downstairs? No? Well she often talks about the **Good** People. Her term for the lost race of people she lived with in medieval Scotland. She thinks she's a time traveller. And Veronica in the flat above her tells anyone who will listen that she was the first Englishwoman to have trans-human sex in low Earth orbit.[3] Her words. I am not breaking any confidences here.*

I shake my head. I have no time for others. There are all sorts of travellers on this bourne, with their own stories – some of them true. Instead I take him on a tour of all the items in my temporary world that could be used to kill, maim or defend, using the angles, edges and textures that make the Human world such a place of mortality. Cushions, pillows, cords. Wires, pens, chairs. Even the red-topped newspaper could be folded, in less than two seconds, into a hard wedge that could dent a skull.

I did not know I lived in such a war zone, sir!

I show him how to use the heel of his hand to strike upward into the base of an attacker's nose. Or the Y of flesh between forefinger and thumb that can be crashed into the wind-pipe to immobilise someone without killing them. None of this nonsense of punching with closed fists. I show him thirty pressure points that, depending on how they were struck, or how hard, can immobilise, paralyse, cause extreme pain or simple death. Easy.

But sir… this piece of cotton thread on the back of chair. Even you could not turn this into a deadly weapon. Could you?

The thread was two inches long.

Easy, I said. *Très facile. You say to your opponent with a stern face: what is this thread doing here? And then when he looks, et puis, you bash his head with a frying pan. Simple.*

As he starts practising on the pillows in my bedroom, visualising them as the heads of his enemies, I slip out of the apartement to continue my quest.

---

3   See *Shimmying Hips*, Kindle e-book, for Veronica's Story

I will tell you another secret. I am scared of women. My mother, the Lady of the Lake, taught me things that might be pure and true for the Faery realm. They are not necessarily true in the world of Humans. Though I am gallant, chivalrous, protective, I am not entirely sure how to relate to the fair sex in either race. Gwenevere so obsessed me that I never learned ordinary skills. There was a woman – Elaine – who tricked me into sleeping with her and became as insane about me as I have been for my Queen. She taught me nothing about everyday human love. I deny that the child is mine.

Eh bien, now I have climbed into the Botanical Gardens and rest quietly among the bizarre shadows of the exotic trees. I sit on a bench and look up at the Milky Way. A few shooting stars hiss across the sky. Is it still Monday? Was it only this morning that Kelvin learned the ABC of fighting? Certainly I have had many brooding thoughts after Compline. Thoughts which serve for me like the ticking of a watch does for Humans. It must be very early on Tuesday.

I am looking for the fées of course. They love starlight and trees, and – unless they come fully into the world – are best seen out of the corner of the eye. I am also remembering. Trying to get clear images. When you walk along the depths of the lake, it can send up clouds of mud. It can disturb creatures. Humans have dumped all sorts of rubbish which lies on the bottom. I see countless skeletons; corpses which still retain rotting flesh, and which sway slightly. I see rusting machineries of war, unexploded shells and even a white car with black paint on one crumpled wing.

It amuses me when I look at pure Humans doing their own remembering. They have a screen in the air, above their brows, and the pictures appear thereon. They look slightly upward when they think and reminisce. Because my thoughts, of my faery self, are composed from within the heart, I must look downward.

I have probably made too much 'noise' in my search for Gwenevere. If I have not worn actual armour, then things in my mind and soul have made loud clanking noises as I have wandered the world. Now I am sitting still, here amid the palms, next to an ornamental Temple of Minerva which, amusingly, flickers with the tall will-o'-the-wisp lights of lesser faeries at play. Like fragments of rainbows in the dark.

I never knew my birth mother. As the years go on I yearn for her. Increasingly.

Nimué was never less than kind, but she also seemed to have an agenda. I have swum through the centuries just wanting simple, uncomplicated loving. Instead I have got Gwenevere. When I walk through the darkened streets of cities and see the people in the doorways wrecked by alcohol or drugs, I wonder if my addiction is not as bad.

Nimué gave me a code of behaviour. She taught me things. Was it a good code? Were they good things? I would never show these doubts toward Sir Bruce. I would simply put down my visor and charge.

A knight should have two hearts, she said. One as hard and impenetrable as diamond. The other as soft and pliable as hot wax. The one which is hard as diamond should oppose those who are treacherous and cruel. For as a diamond cannot be polished, so a knight should be fierce and cruel toward the Bad People who do their best to damage and destroy justice. And as soft, hot wax can be shaped and made to do whatever you wish, in the same way good and compassionate people should be able to lead the knight to everything gracious and gentle. But… he should take good care that the heart of wax is not accessible to those who are cruel and treacherous, for any good he might do them would be utterly wasted.

Her words. Are they true? Can a man have two hearts like this? Was she talking about an ideal of Human and Faery conjoined? I have been responsible for so much death that my own heart is clearly of the diamond. Vraiment. It is only when I come near Gwenevere that I can sense the soft and pliable heart beating quickly beneath all my scars.

Perhaps if I sit quietly she will come to me.

The night sky above is calm. I can almost hear the stars singing, as the pure fées can. In the trees, bushes and shrubs around me – exotic and so much like a jungle – I can hear hares and badgers, owls and nightjars. The tiny stream tumbles away in stages down from the supposedly fake Temple of Minerva which would quickly come alive if any humans troubled themselves to light a few flames.

Come to me, I hear a voice call in my head. *Come to me quickly!*

My heart pounds. It is Gwenevere! Although she sounds more teasing than troubled, that was always her way with me. I stand up and look around. I start to move and almost fall over the bent, dark figure of Ahasuerus who fits between the passing moments like a sigh.

Stay, he says.

I look around. I put my hand over his sour mouth to silence him. He scrapes his clubbed feet over the gravel and shakes himself free. He is a bent shadow, an ancient man wearing one of the duffel coats that the English favour. And he is angry with me.

You've been avoiding me, your oldest friend.

I have – and I was never your friend, I say, looking around, straining all my senses for any hint of my White Shadow. Yet she is gone. Again. She was always a tease. I rescued her so often from situations that were no more than tests or even taunts.

Stay, says the Wandering Jew.

No, I tell him. I have heard all his stories.

Ahasuerus – pah! A powerful name for a pitiful wretch. His story began long before mine. Centuries. I think he was a shoe-maker. Or a baker. He saw the Man Jesus carrying his cross and he laughed. Scorned. Mocked. Jesus looked up from under his crown of thorns and cursed him: to wander the Earth until the Second Coming. That is the story. It is merde. Perhaps.

Gwenevere often babbled about the White Christ, as she called him, as if he was a close relative. That was one thing about her that irritated me. She was on a mission. Always. I wanted her mission to be me. I have fought many wars that were started in the name of Jesus and killed many deserving Bad People. To me, Jesus was just a man. Half the Faery kind thought the same. Some of them tried to rescue her from her folly. In some ways this Man Jesus had cursed them both.

So I have known him as Ahasuerus, Matathias, Buttadeus, Paul Marrane and Isaac Laquedem. As the centuries went by, he would change his name as others would change their clothes.

I didn't mean to say that to Him he started. How often had I heard that! My heart sank. The sense I had of Gwenevere being near had suddenly gone. I could have killed him – if he had not been partly immortal. He admired me for some reason. Perhaps because I was nearly as old as he. If he knew that most of my long life I have felt like a little boy, he would have sought other company.

The sense of my Queen's immanence faded. The sickle moon went behind sudden clouds. This had gone on long enough.

I can set you free, I told him, with the pure tones of absolute truth.

His eyes were two points of light within the hood.

It was just the son of a man you scorned. Not the Son of Man. There were over three hundred other Messiahs touting for business at the same time. He was just a man. I, the great du Lac, tell you this. Try, just for one heartbeat, to believe this. Pretend to believe me. Ask: 'what if...' Try, and you can go home...

The cowl looked up at me in silence. His emotions rolled over like a dice: six dots of anger, four of disbelief, then one of the possibility. The lights of his ancient pupils narrowed and then flared. Ripples in a pond. Then faded. He gasped. Stumbled against me. I pulled away from a hand which had become a claw.

As I walked along the crunching gravel of the path his pitiful figure sank to its knees. Whether in prayer, thanks, or the beginnings of his death throes, I could not say.

Sir Bruce was waiting for me when I got back. Sitting alone in the shadows of my *apartement* – which he seemed to think was his. Something that he owned. I will tell you more about him.

I have known him kill, rape and pillage for his own selfish desires, and then beg for mercy under the chivalric system. He has learned to play all systems throughout the ages, whether they are to do with welfare or legal justice. He breaks the laws, then uses the laws to save himself.

Pax? he says.

Pax I must respond.

He wore blue jeans, a red t-shirt and a light jacket. With training shoes. Immature. His hair was dishevelled, probably from rough sex with the Sally Hart woman who lives below. Yet his face was alight. As if he had found his own Grail in one of the back-streets of Bath.

The reading glasses were high above his brow, like a visor, and he waved a book at me. Paperback. The pages were marked with little sticky notelets that fluttered like feathers. He waved it as I might wave a Danish axe. The air rippled with his excitement. The book was *Lancelot of the Lake*. I told you before, did I not, that I knew the book well. Most of it was lies, some of it was wrong. The few truths were only half-truths. Even these half-truths were twisted. I watched the idiot writing it, centuries ago. Breathless, he even told parts of it to me, the actual du Lac, and him never guessing. He thought me crass for laughing. He thought I envied his knowledge of letters.

The girl mis-heard you but I didn't. Not Dulux but du Lac.

I said nothing. I played chess. The patterns of the pieces comfort me. I imagine that Gwenevere is moving the other pieces. I think she does. The only other explanation is subsidence! She is in my head. Toujours.

I will warn you that Sir Bruce has a weapon which digs between the ribs. It causes more blood loss and damage than anything I have ever wielded. It is called charm. And lies. Charming lies.

Sir Bruce is not immortal but he is 'of a kind.' In every age and every life there is a Sir Bruce sans Pitié. They often marry worthy women and cause them much grief. Undeserved. I wonder if this McHaffee, as he calls himself, has truly forgotten Who he is.

You believe you're Lancelot.

What ignorance! I am 'of the Lake'. A small droplet of something that is deep and cold and pure. Lancelot was always a false name. My mothers never called me that.

I turn the board, saying nothing. I think of Gwenevere and move a piece. Sometimes they move themselves. Other times I have to help. The 'doctor' looks up from his book which is filled with comments in red ink in the margins and frowns.

There is no king, he said. *That move you made with the knight made no sense. Either you don't know the rules or you're trying to tell me something.*

Bien sûr! I was playing the Faery Chess. It is about creating patterns, restoring harmonies. Responding to impulses from the other world. We had our own especial rules, Gwenevere and I.

And the word GAW you uttered when they saved you from the weir. It was Gorre wasn't it? The kingdom of Gorre?

Yes I offered, throwing him a tiny clue that would both inform and distract.

He sat back triumphant

Then you are Lancelot. Pardon me – you believe that you are Lancelot!

No, I said simply.

He sat forward, bewildered. He could see my truth.

Listen, don't piss me about, just answer honestly – honestly – one simple little question. Do you believe, or have you ever even briefly believed, that you are Lancelot.

I looked him powerfully in the eye. I have stopped runaway horses and mad bishops with this look. *No*, I said. *I have never. Ever. Believed that I am, was, or ever will be Lancelot.*

You're impenetrable he said, after a long pause and evil glare. It was not meant as praise.

I am. He would have to find his own long, thin-bladed misericord to strike me where he wanted.

He stood up. The chair fell over and he left it. *I've had enough of this crap 'Mr Dulux'. I've got other people more deserving than you. People who want my help. I'll see myself out* he sneered, as I continued with my game.

The door slammed after him. Petulant. Sir Bruce sans Pitié has never changed.

I was sitting outside the Abbey on one of the benches that line the great expanse before the doors. They were having a special service for one of the last survivors of the Great War. There were boy soldiers and toy soldiers lined up to salute his coffin. I sat quietly, thinking. Calmly, deeply. Out of the corners of my eyes and sometimes directly, I scanned the windows of the shops around and the unfriendly Pump Room where Sir Bruce caused such havoc. No sign of Gwenevere. A hint of blonde, a hint of silver, from other Humans. No hint of the starlight which flows through her.

I saw him approach from behind. Kelvin. My Squire. He is sensitive to my needs and although I did not actually summon, nevertheless he arrived. Very good.

Hey listen to this Mich – er Sir. You won't – I mean you will not – believe this!

Why do you speak in such a stilted manner? Are you French?

His mouth opened and closed. *Because… ah… you told me to do so a few days ago. You told me not to elide words.*

The world has turned since. Speak in your normal way from now on.

His brows furrowed. He felt that I was 'take the mickey' again, as he termed it. Or was that Sir Bruce? The young squire sighed and continued. Not realising I had been testing him.

Okay. Well, look at this…

'This' was an article in the newspaper. A student jape. Someone had stolen a mummy – an actual Egyptian mummy – from a museum or a private collection, somewhere, and left it sitting in the little Temple of Minerva in the Botanical Gardens.

What sort of nutter would do that?! he squeaked in delight.

He was about to say more but he caught my mood. Perhaps remembering his own contract – or was it an oath? – he sat quietly next to me.

What a nightmare, yah? he said, nodding toward the unmournful mourners. *The war I mean.*

What did he know about nightmares? What did he know about war? Thanks to me, and a million like me, he had known no war in his lifetime. No terror. No sudden death. No despair.

My great-grandfather was at the Somme. He said it was like a wasteland.

So was I. It was more than that.

What, on an excursion? Before you came here?

I took a deep breath and closed my eyes. Sitting upright. Palms on thighs. The Somme... the very word is like the first drum-beat of an execution. It clutches my ancient heart of wax. I had seen death in all its forms before 1916 but the Somme... thoughts, words fail. If there was ever an argument for the Faery races to shun all contact with the Human, it was there.

I will not try to describe the Wasteland fully because no-one can. It is not part of my story. Yet I remember a dark night in Mametz Wood when I went to help a fine young officer in the Royal Welch Fusiliers. He had done bold things against his natural inclination. He had helped his men. I knew that he could not wear his gas mask because of his broken nose. I knew that he was exhausted, and wounded.

They called it a wood. Zut! There was no foliage anywhere, not a single leaf. The trees were fishbones. The bones had flesh dangling from them. All around were craters filled with stagnant mud, oil, dead horses and dead men. Stinking. Bloated corpses. From the British lines behind us, carried on the wind, came the reek of latrines, rotting sandbags, fumes of phosphorus, sulphur, lyddite and cordite and chloride of lime. Decomposing bodies everywhere, left to rot without dignity. Their uniforms full of frayed holes, like moth-eaten blankets. The ground was strewn with shell cases, bones, and shattered skulls like crowns.

The young man was sitting against a tree. His spark was almost gone. The full moon was our enemy, exposing, pinning us to the degraded world of dying humanity.

He fell forward. I pulled him. For du Lac, a creature of earth and water, the mud was always an ally. I dragged him by the belt, sliding him between the craters. I knew that *I* would not die. I did not want him to.

We got into a trench. Safe.

Old Gravy's been hit! cried someone. *Get the medic! Get a stretcher!*

Thanks he said to me, nodding. I told him to hang on. Help would come to him soon. Shells exploded nearby. They were almost beautiful. He was too tired to flinch. The moon went behind clouds. German flares went up. We close our eyes out of habit and training, waiting until the flare drops so that we can see better through the darkness when it has expired. To one side, not seeing us, the German machine-gun bullets go *phut phut phut, phut phut phut.*

What keeps you going? he gasped. *King and Country?* I admired his pluck. His despair was a heavy chain mail yet he still had that fragment of curiosity that makes poets and heroes.

I sat back on the fire step and felt the damp earth soak through to my spine.

I have a lady beyond compare, I confessed. *And I have loved her an exceedingly long time.*

Do you have a photograph?

I pointed up to the stars.

He thought I was pointing to the German flares. Taking a handkerchief from his pocket he tried to wipe his face, coughing badly as he did so.

A lady? You make her sound aristocratic.

She is of the stars.

Then she is very high born. A queen indeed. I envy you.

He spat and coughed more. There was blood in the phlegm. He was fading. He would not fade.

I wish I had someone to keep me going. Through all this…

He gave a wide gesture with his bandaged hand. As if in response the British cannons returned fire on the Germans.

Perhaps, I said, *if you start searching for your own bright and white goddess you might help others find theirs.*

I stood up, but still crouching, keeping my head well below the parapet. The German snipers with their Mausers were very good. There were others who needed me that night

I don't understand.

I must go now and say goodbye to all this. But look for the roebuck in the thicket and one day, Captain Robert Graves, you will certainly understand…

Sir? Sir? You drifted off. Dr McHaffee said he felt you had occasional petit mals.

I opened my eyes. There were jongleurs and minstrels plying their trade, someone else was attempting what seemed to be a yodelled version of Nessun Dorma. I sighed and shook my head. The gravity of the Somme can even pull down someone like du Lac. I had to struggle to get to my own surface.

The man is fool. When your contract with him ends, you can take an oath and work for me.

He laughed. *You're pulling my leg, Michael. Sir. Yah? He's going to make me redundant soon anyway. The funding for Tigh Aisling is running out. The higher powers aren't convinced. He takes it personally.*

Then work for me now. For two weeks.

I could see bewilderment and disbelief in his young features. He could see sincerity and honesty in mine – so very different to what he had been getting from Sir Bruce.

What would I do? More importantly, how could you pay me?

You will help me find someone. Will this be enough?

I handed him a large bundle of money.

Christ! he swore, looking at it. That was good. With that sort of interjection he would be perfect bait to attract Gwenevere. *Christ!* he said again, unnecessarily loud. Unacceptably indiscreet. I had to shove the notes into the top pocket of his jacket. A light went on in his face. Understanding.

Oh. Em. Gee. he said, in that unfathomable code that so many youngsters use. *I heard it on the radio this morning. Two men who robbed the Royal Crescent Hotel were themselves robbed by someone and left half crippled on the cobblestones until the police came. That was you!*

I shook my head. He read this act as a denial. It was actually exasperation at the men's behaviour. They were not half crippled. They were not even a quarter crippled. I gave them every chance to stop. Every chance to give me the money in an act of loving kindness. They swore. They compared me to a part of female anatomy. They tried to head-butt me – du Lac! – with their crash helmets.

The money in his pocket almost glowed. His face certainly did. Potentials! It was the same look I saw on the faces of the knights in Camelot when they thought they might win the Holy Grail. I am sure most of them – Sir Kay in particular – would have sold it to the first Saracen they met, for as much as they could possibly procure.

You attract trouble, don't you?

This excited him. Twitched his hips on the bench next to me. Inelegant. At last, his job was no longer boring. At last, he no longer had to be paid to care.

Squire Kelvin, light a candle in your room tonight and leave the window open and the curtains pulled wide. All sorts of nightlife will flutter toward the flame. Because I am 'of the light' I draw toward me all sorts of wrong-doers. Bad People.

He laughed. I could not see why. I have never fully understood the layered humour of Humans. Iron I know, and wear it as armour. Irony – as they call it – is beyond me.

Now here is some more money. Do not look at me like that. Look straight ahead, conceal it quickly. And by the way… your eye shadow clashes badly with your shirt. Choose a light tone. Now, maintenant, I want you to go and buy us two palfreys.

What's a palfrey?

I had to think. Had to remember which world I was living in, and why, and when.

To me a palfrey is a horse. A quality beast that is fitting for squires and ladies. Not quite as expensive or powerful as the destriers that I would ride into battle upon. I think you would call it a motor bike. I have two crash helmets that will fit us. Perfectly…

I am swimming – very slowly – in the pool at the Sports Centre. I am, of course, 'like a fish' as the English would say to describe my prowess. Most of the time I swim around on the bottom to hide my scars from the poor wretches who might be appalled. I do not actually have gills, but I can stay under for long periods. It makes the lifeguards anxious.

My allocated time seems to be up, but I am not going to vacate the pool yet. For a moment between sessions I have the waters to myself. I relax. Gwenevere would never come here. She could not stand the chlorine. Or the exposure. I will see her soon. I am beginning to hear the song in my blood that means she is near. It has been a long time since I have heard it. Mercifully, I am a soldier. Love is like a soldier's commitment to his men, or country: it makes it easier to carry on.

I float on my back, on the surface. I dream, I remember…

What was Camelot like?

It was a place of thin, gleaming sky-reaching towers which defied gravity, soaring walls of white gold, every window filled with pure and perfect stained glass, golden-yellow cobbles in the many courtyards. There were no weeds, no broken masonry and a kind of stillness about the place which made it seem as if it were in a bell-jar. The only sounds were the sounds of laughter, learned but respectful debate, manly jousts in which no-one was ever really hurt. All the women were beautiful, no-one ever had bowel movements and there was bird-song at the appropriate times.

You have all been there. Truly. Not just to Winchester, Colchester, Cadbury or Carlisle and all the other places that claim to have been the 'true' Camelot. It does not matter that the reality is one of rough-hewn timbers, drafty halls, crude moats and rickety defences, the whole area for half a league around stinking with the shit thrown over the walls. Plague-ridden, dark. Beggars like flies. Miserable. The Shining Place is within you. I have been taken there on the eve of many battles when the frightened soldier, so ready to do his duty, would yarn and almost turn his sad little home town into a hymn of beauty, his bleak childhood a forest of marvels, his hag of a mother a creature from heaven.

With such remembrance, inspired by such fear, we all come from Camelot.

My foster mother, the Lady of the Lake, talked of little else when I was growing up. No place was more perfect, no aim was loftier than becoming a knight serving Arthur. I believed her. As only a boy who loves his mother can. Trusting. Had I known, then, that she had stolen me from my *true* mother, I might have seen through her words. The older I get, the more it does seem as if she was unhinged. Like Gwenevere, she appeared to have her own mission. I, whose rank in the world since has never been higher than private, was never privy to the secrets through which I swam.

She and her followers taught me to fight from the earliest age. I was good at it. I was great! I enjoyed fighting. She taught me that every part of the knight's apparel had significance. Especially the sword! She, who had no husband or lover that I was aware of, would speak softly and earnestly whenever she lectured about the sword.

This weapon is the most honourable and the most noble, she said, and the one with most dignity. She taught me how to cut right and left with the two edges. With one edge I would be servant and defender of the people; with the other I would be an avenger of wrongs done to the Most High. I begin to think she meant herself. But the point of the sword… Oh she loved that lesson best. She said that the point rightly signifies obedience, for it stabs, and nothing so stabs the heart – not loss of land nor of wealth – as being forced to obey. Never once did I think to ask her what she meant by that. It is not right that a boy should question his mother's sex life. Although, it must be said, the sex lives of the Faery kind are not quite as simple as that of Humans.

She even named my sword for me: Seure, which she said meant Sequence.

Even now I do not understand what she was trying to tell me. Something to do with Time and its patterns that so obsesses the Faery world. I blooded the sword against the Bad People at Saxon Rock and the world was never the same again.

However I am not quite sure what my Lady of the Lake would have made of the Short Magazine Lee Enfield, the Projector, Infantry Anti Tank, or the Heckler and Koch SA80 assault rifles with which I plied my trade in later centuries.

But how do you get to be a presence in Camelot – a Knight of the Round Table? You have to be a pretty boy. Well built. Noble features. Chic. Good family background. That is, aristrocratic. As the Humans understand aristocracy. From accepted families. That was all. It was much the same during what they call the Great War. At least among the British. Eton? Harrow? Your father an Earl did you say? Then here is your officer's uniform. Go away and lead. No training needed. It is in the blood!

Merde! At least we French had been preparing for years. The British started off as amateurs. They improved slowly, as more blood was shed into the soil of Flanders. I helped them as best I could. I think it might have been du Lac who summoned the angels at Mons.

Read what the chroniclers wrote about Camelot. They got it right. All the lesser kings and their queens wanted their boys to get into the court. What started off as a brilliant idea by Merlin, developed by Arser when he still had balls, degenerated into farce. There were times when he and Gwenevere, in exasperation, would arrange Quests, or tests and challenges just to stop them spending all their time in the Great Hall telling each other how goodly they were and polishing their cod-pieces. I tried to keep apart from all that. Was I, du Lac, the greatest and most powerful knight simply because the rest were such in-bred drips?

I hope to meet the fat Merlin soon to ask him these things, for I am becoming troubled.

And the Round Table? That belonged to Gwenevere. It was her father's before her. In truth it was more concept than reality, although she did bring a wooden piece of furniture with her from Lyonesse. Not grand. A kind of a flat-pack that could be assembled. A lot of the Swedish furniture in my little apartement is made up from thus. She wanted the Human and the Faery races to balance, to blend, to mate. It was never going to happen. Jamais. Not in my lifetime. Then again, in the faery realms, they have no sense of time as Humans do. And I have had a very long lifetime.

In those days, in the great depths of the Time before Time a few of the Folk, like Gwenevere, learned how to step between the worlds. Rarely was it the other way. Many of the Human race were scared of them: lordly and beautiful they seemed. With cold hearts. Shining – and clean! Every king wanted a faery for his queen. Every king lusted for the dazzling whiteness of the faery blood. Gwenevere could, and did, go from one world to the other. At will. I, du Lac, had no such easy skill. I blame my Human mother for that.

Pax! shouts Sir Bruce, breaking to my reveries. *Come on, I'm playing your stupid game! Pax!*

I take a deep breath and allow myself to sink to the very bottom of the pool. I look up. He has taken his shoes off, rolled up his trousers and is sitting on the edge waiting for me, his scrofulous feet dangling in the water. I stay under long enough to make him anxious. I send bubbles up. Teasing. Three lifeguards and a policeman are hovering next to him, blurred waving shapes as the world above is seen from the world below. He gestures them away. They sway, they go. I surface, slowly. Smiling.

Who the fuck are you? he asks. He is asking it in a different way this time. He means not Who, but What. Perhaps.

He is wearing a grey three piece suit. White shirt and grey tie. The sort of thing men wear today when they are involved in daily office jousting.

I say nothing. I give him a gracious smile, such as my foster mother taught.

Please… Anything but this dumb silence. Use your Franglais on me if you want. Young Kelvin speaks it all the time now. He seems to have developed a dangerous transference onto you. Especially after your wild rides on the stolen motorbikes last night. I had to sack him.

Franglais? Does Sur Bruce not remember the old High French that was used in all the courts? I must praise Kelvin. He works for me now. Sir Bruce has not yet realised. Time passes him by as it never does for me. Time merely circulates gently within the boundaries of my lake, like currents from unseen streams.

I am naked before you Sir Bruce. Nothing concealed. Rien. Strike your hardest blow. Finish me at last.

I think he wanted to spit into the waters – my waters – but the armour he wore created by thick sheaves of Health and Safety Regulations stopped him, lips pursed, frozen before the act. To be fair, that was an echo of the old knightly code which still muttered in his human blood: a knight should not, for fear of death, do anything which can be seen as shameful. Rather, he should be more afraid of shame than suffering death. He swallowed his bile. Glared at me. A great lance of hatred aiming straight at my face.

You know that Kelvin was classed as a Vulnerable Adult until I helped him?

With me, he is now Invulnerable.

Are you having a relationship?

I swim to the side and say nothing. Bien sûr we are having a relationship: he is my Squire. He tends to my basic needs. I am teaching him courtly things. He will help me find Gwenevere. I will make sure he never goes anywhere near the frauds of Camelot.

*You **are** having a relationship!* yells Sir Bruce, using a different angle of attack as I leave the pool area. I can hear his bare feet slapping on the tiles as he hurries to catch up with me. There is desperation in the sound. He stands in front of me, at the door to the changing rooms. He is seething.

Two days ago Tigh Aisling was faced with closure. The directors and funding authorities had decided they would no longer support it. All my work down the drain. Then I had a visit. From the legal firm Harris and Dunne. Two very sinister young men who assured me that funding would be provided. And more. The caveat being that I had to continue treating you. There is no such firm as Harris and Dunne. Yet Tigh Aisling's accounts are bulging. And when I contacted the police I was –

The young policeman whom I first hefted around in the Union Passage, and then admired my prowess at the station, approached me, almost elbowing Sir Bruce to one side. Clearly the young man was learning to use his weight to better advantage.

Sir, he says to me, handing me a towel. *You really shouldn't swim naked in public places. There is actually a law against it.*

He speaks courteously, kindly. I nod and cover myself.

The world keeps changing m'sieur, I tell him.

Can we offer you a lift anywhere sir?

This is too much for my pitiful nemesis.

You're fucking protecting him, seethes Sir Bruce to the constable. *Who is he?*

The young knight – for he cannot be anything but with all this armour, his oath to serve, and his goodly manner – ignores him. He leads me toward my clothes and offers them as I dress.

As we leave, Sir Bruce might have followed, spitting with fury and unanswered mysteries, but I offer the simplest yet most effective of attacks: I throw his expensive leather shoes into the deep end. They sink as if they are made of lead.

Really sir, asks the policeman when we get out onto the street and no one is likely to listen. *Who are you?*

I am du Lac, I tell him. *One day I will show you more effective ways of using that truncheon. You will never have to use a taser or a pepper spray again.*

He smiles. Hugely.

The motorbikes were not stolen. They were paid for honestly with money taken from Bad People. The ride was not wild. Squire Kelvin was barely able to master his palfrey even though, at 50cc, it was clearly designed for older ladies. Mine, a destrier, was ten times as powerful. Japanese. We made an odd couple as we rode. Proceeding slowly, in fits and starts. Myself, had I been alone, I would have ridden hard, spurring it like a demon. For Kelvin's sake, we rode sedately. The first lesson a Squire must learn is self-control.

We cruised around the very rich places that had been built upon and sometimes into, the encircling hills. The moon was full. It was mocking. Its light was blue-silvery, like my lake at dusk. On the high encircling places it shone bright as day. The street lights of the little city looked like strings of jewels dumped into a bowl.

You seem to enjoy wearing your helmet! he cried.

Of course I did. It was so much like the many helms I wore in my prime. Was that yesterday? Or centuries before? I am not sure. He was impressed, I feel, by the ostrich plume I had fastened on to give it authenticity. Veracity.

I haven't had this much fun in years… he added. Very wistful.

He took me around the kingdom of Gorre. I would call it Questing if the word did not give me such unpleasant memories of the poseurs in Camelot. I was – bien sûr – looking for Gwenevere. Putting myself out into the world so that she could find me. We rode slowly through Bath's 7 crescents: Lansdown, Camden, Royal, Cavendish, Widcome, Norfolk and the half-crescent called Somerset.

I was looking for clues. Something to tell me where a White Shadow might be hiding herself, or kept prisoner. She would never, through choice, stay anywhere common. She is a Queen. Nor would any kidnapper risk imprisoning her anywhere ordinary. She is a Faery. Also a terrible snob with respect to both roles. I simply speak the truth. It does not diminish my love.

Once, police stopped us. Perhaps it was the erratic nature of

Kelvin's progress. We were not speeding. I, du Lac, obey the laws. Usually. It looked as though they might arrest us but one of them got a message on his radio, furrowed his monobrow, whispered to his companion, and they stepped aside.

Kelvin glowed. I, being a King's son, accept this as the norm.

With his knowledge of the town, he also took us around the seven hills which surround the town like frozen waves: Beechen Cliff and Southdown, Kelston Round Hill and Lansdown, Solsbury Hill and Bathford Hill. And Bathampton Down. It was not scenery I wanted, but song. I would stop at the spot where I could find the oldest stone, remove my helmet and press my brow lightly against it.

Kelvin was amused. *You're like one a them Indians who put their ears to the ground to hear buffalo. What are you actually doing? Sir?*

I did not try to explain. Sometimes the earth can vibrate – give out its own holy hymn – when the fées are near. That night – silence. Apart from Kelvin's gentle laughter. He is a jolly soul despite all the tortures that Sir Bruce must have inflicted.

Then, catching the light of the moon, I glimpsed a tall, thin, square tower. My heart gave a leap when I saw the dome of gold on the topmost gilded lantern which was so much like the one at the Temple of Diana Nemorensis at Lake Nemi. Where I was taken often as a child by Nimué. The sense of remembrance was so strong that for a moment I almost felt her presence.

Do you know that place? asked Kelvin, seeing my shock.

I went there as a boy, I said softly to myself alone. He thought I meant this tower.

Yah. Me too. Went on a school trip. It's called Beckford's Tower. Built by some tosser who had orgies there. They dangled me down the stairwell by my ankles when the useless teachers weren't looking.

He was babbling. He was troubled. So was I. Nostalgia is a terrible blade for self-inflicted wounds. When I was a boy, at every August Full Moon, Nimué would lead me through the sacred grove, along a shimmering procession of torches and candles around the dark waters of lake known as Diana's Mirror. The lights of their candles joined the light of the moon, dancing on the surface of the still water, dancing in my foster-mother's eyes. She told me in a tone that brooked no disagreement, whispering excitedly:

We worship Diana of the Hunt.

She is also known of old as Artemis, and Selene, and dark Hekate.

Only human blood can appease her. And we honour hounds because of Diana's role as goddess of the hunt.

Even so, I du Lac do not like dogs, as I think I told you, even if they are hounds.

I did not understand much of what she told me. I was a little boy. Un petit garçon from a distant land. I did not understand that the small written messages on ribbons, tied to trees, were requests and offerings to the Goddess. Nor that the small baked statuettes of body parts in need of healing, or the clay images of mother and child and the many tiny sculptures of stags were also part of their supplication.

Have an apple, King's Son, she said to me and watched me eating that which she had plucked from the orchard, as if the apple were more than apple, and the orchard more than a place of trees.

One day my Handsome Foundling, you will be Rex Nemorensis here, the King of the Grove. You will hold this position until someone comes along to defeat you. The death of the Rex has to be violent. The spouting blood of the loser will fertilise the ground. But no-one will ever best you for I will make you the greatest knight in the world. This lake will become my lake and Diana Nemorensis is our goddess, looking down fondly on us both, ensuring the succession of kings.

She said that every year. It was almost her prayer. I did not understand one half of it. I know now she was unbalanced.

Sir? Sir! General Dulux. Sir! You've drifted off again said Kelvin, not unkindly, tapping my helmet.

I was merely looking at the cinema screen before my heart, as I have explained. I was never more intensely awake.

What month is it Squire?

August. Why?

I put spurs to my charger and roared toward that tower.

The place was neither handsome nor elegant. It had two large squat buildings at the base and the tower rising from them. The proportions of all were unpleasing. It spoke of Mysteries rather than style. Exactly the sort of place I might expect to find messages from the otherworld. Had it been near the sea, the tower would have made a fine lighthouse. Next to it was a large graveyard which, in the moonlight, showed off the headstones with almost sinister beauty.

Figures moved among the tombs. Not the undead but the unalive folks with matted hair and dreadlocks and scrawny dogs, disturbed by us from their slumbers. They kept well away. Respectful. I do not know what they saw in me.

Dulux said one, his voice crisp and clear in the night air. They could not move on from calling me this instead of du Lac. Yet what is this paint but a more viscous type of liquid? One that will stay where they apply it. One they could use and create light with. Of the light.

I'm not going in there said Kelvin, though I had not asked him. *Looks like summat from a Hammer Horror Film.*

I went forward and despite his words he followed me anyway. Hanging onto my surcoat. Without knowing it, he had actually passed a small test. The grave of this Monsieur Beckford, the creator, was very strange. Set on an oval mound in an oval hollow. So much like a faery barrow. Was Beckford a fée? Or mixed race like myself? When the soul of a fée enters the foetus of a Human before birth they can struggle. Like a radio that is not quite tuned-in. They can behave oddly. Badly. Bizarrely. And often they have more grace than Humans will ever achieve.

A nutter said Kelvin out loud. *Definitely a nutter.*

I assumed he meant Beckford.

It was odd, this grave. Did it carry a message? For whom? The tomb itself was a large sarcophagus of pink polished granite with bronze armorial plaques. There were words engraved. I studied them intensely:

"Enjoying humbly the most precious gift of heaven to man – Hope."

I nodded. I liked this corpse. He died in 1844. Had I met him in my travels? And there was a poem on the other side:

A Prayer:
Eternal Power!
Grant me, through obvious clouds one transient gleam
Of thy bright essence in my dying hour.

Gwenevere had played such games with me in the past, tested me in so many ways that I look for her spirit in all such things. I sometimes ponder that her symbol should not be the chessboard but the maze. When she was with Arser her pennons always had an azure field and three gold crowns. Meaningless. Diplomatic. I dreamed of the day when she could boldly display the white field with bend gules that is my own device.

Let's go inside said Kelvin. The shadows of the graveyard dead seemed to be troubling him.

The large double doors were locked. No lights. I would have ridden my charger right through them but my squire surprised me.

Allow me, he offered. *Don't look, then they can't blame you.*

With his back turned toward me he fumbled at the lock with a tool of some sort, plus a strip of plastic. The door creaked open.

Entrez! he said, using the High French I had been teaching him.

I who am not easily impressed was impressed.

With an arch look he leaned toward me and whispered: *I am your keyworker after all.*

Where did you learn that?

I went to a boarding school for troubled boys. I learned thievery, mischievery, how to pick locks on old heaps like this. Yah and lots of buggery whether I wanted it or not.

I frowned.

Yah, well, you had to be a faery or a freak to survive in a place like that. Me, I was both.

I looked at him. One slightly raised eyebrow. Was he 'taking the Michael' as they called it? No. He was serious. Sad. I think he needed a mother.

Allons I said, giving him a brief manly clap to the shoulder that almost knocked him down. Then led the way.

The place echoed with misery and torment. At its best it had felt little joy. It needed every room and every artefact painted white, like my apartement. That might help. I made my companion stay in the miserable hallway while I went from room to room ready for combat in each one. I once heard a human mutter the phrase 'same old same old' and that was exactly right. How often had I done this, through how many centuries? Still, it was necessary.

Isn't this a bit Oh Tee Tee Captain Dulux sir?

He did not – yet – understand the simplest principles of crossing ground under fire. My actions were vital. Booby-traps were always a possibility.

Clear. We went up to the first floor.

The museum said Kelvin.

The place was filled with statues – dead human heads preserved in stone. If the holy places around Lake Nemi were filled with those small statues of body parts that needed healing, what did these marble heads make pleas for?

That one looks like you. Sir.

Non. Not so handsome. His chin was quite weak. Brow too low. I said nothing witty in reply but continued to explore, using the corners of my eyes, relaxing into vision. We came to a long narrow room fitted out as an oratory, where the paintings were all devotional. Dead love between dead people. A marble Virgin and Child stood bathed in moonlight from a cunning skylight. It reminded me of Nimué and myself.

Then there was the spiral stairwell which led up to the gilded belvedere. It was so much like the inside of a shell. Or the eye and its iris. Captains Graves or Sassoon could have told me which was the better image had they still been alive.

We climbed the stairs, widdershins. The view around was magnifique. The surrounding hills and the country beyond rolled and crashed gently under the moonlight like waves. This land-locked tower really did function like a lighthouse.

Tell me what I see, squire…

Well, on a clear day that way, you can see King Alfred's Tower at Stourhead. There and there – you'd see the two White Horse monuments at Westbury and Cherhill. To the north, the Forest of Dean and to the west across the Bristol Channel you can see into Wales.

What are those lights there? There? And there…

University. Admiralty. Admiralty. And yet more Admiralty offices.

Admiralty? We are a long way from the sea.

Biggest employer in Bath, the Admiralty. I'm sure there's a joke in that somewhere: The whole of Royal Navy is controlled from a Bath. Or maybe you can fit the whole of the Royal Navy into a bath these days, after all the cuts.

He wandered off. Back down to the museum. He did not have a head for heights. I had the panorama to myself. Well, not quite to myself. I started looking out the corners of my eyes again. I knew she would be here somewhere, somehow. I had the forget-me-nots sealed in plastic and then stuck over my heart with duct tape. When

I put my hand over the patch I can feel the beats. I am not sure if this comes from the systole and diastole of my pumping blood or the flower itself, pulsing in tune with Gwenevere's love. It is very pleasing.

Sssssh she whispered. I shivered. I had almost forgotten what her voice sounded like. *Don't turn, don't try to look.*

Fées as advanced as she could leave their bodies and visit in dreams. Maintaining contact was like balancing a sword by its point on the fingertip. I closed my eyes, swaying slightly, and built up her image in my imagination to help the contact. To salve myself.

I felt her breath, gentle as star-light, on the right side of my neck just above the collar. It was the place I always loved her kissing me. Tender. Silent. I swayed. The gentility of her loving could unseat me in ways that Sir Bruce with his lance, sword and mace never could.

You will find me soon.
Where?
You will release me.
How?
We will be together.
When?
Forever.

It was too much. I spun on my heel, turned. The floorboards creaked like small-bore pistols and she disappeared.

Are you okay? asked Kelvin who had clearly had enough of this adventure. *I heard you muttering and came back.*

He put his hands out to steady me. Me!

Let's get you home he offered, leading the way.

That is all I have ever wanted. I gave some money to the wretches waiting outside with their silent, quivering dogs. One of them I remembered from before. In the Union Passage. A man with silver rings in his eyebrows, studs in his lips, nose and ears. I remembered the dank smell of earth. He saluted me as I walked past. I think, as Kelvin might have said, he was taking the Michael.

When I came home, back to my white monastic cell, I wanted to cry. Instead I remembered Nimué's advice: Do not devote your heart to a love which makes you grow indolent, but to one which makes you improve, for a heart which becomes indolent through love cannot achieve noble things, for it does not dare.

I was never indolent.

It is Thursday today. All day, as my squire jokes in that clumsy English way of his. Kelvin is not around at the moment. I am a modern employer. I give my Squires time to themselves. He said he was off to do some cottaging, whatever that might be.

I am sitting in the top floor of the café known as Sally Lunn's. It has a pale and cramped interior on three levels. Real flowers in plastic vases. The people who were in here left when they saw me. I think they might have been Bad People, who knew to leave when they could. I reassured the jolie young waitress that she would have no trouble now and ordered half a toasted and buttered Sally Lunn Bun topped with 3 scrambled eggs from happy chickens plus a large tea for one. She noticed that I spilled a little tea when I poured. I explained that I am exquisitely sensitive to the vibrations of passing traffic.

I read the pamphlet which tells the history of the tea room. It says that, according to legend, a young Huguenot refugee – Solange Luyon – came to Bath in 1680 after escaping persecution in France. To win friends and find employment she began baking a rich, brioche bun similar to the French festival breads. No one could pronounce her name properly. She answered to Sally Lunn.

Nonsense. I rode near here with Arser once. Not into Aquae Sulis as they called it then but a little north. Was this the great battle of Badon? I cannot remember. Yet we were here. Almost. They still cooked the buns that had been sold to the Legions. You could buy a large round one called a Sol, like the sun. Or a demi called Lune, after the moon. Or, for a discount, you could have both by asking for a Sol et Lune. Obvious.

An atmosphere rises up the stairs. Splashes into my nostrils. It is not sulphurous but holds dark associations. A smell of old seaweed and salt, wet rocks, wet sand and damp air. Green, blue, darkest grey, broken by strips of white. A fathomless and seductive breeze.

Well well well comes the familiar woman's voice. *Well well well and bloody **well**! If it isn't the great –*

Arrêtez! That makes seven times that you have said it so it must be true. Do you mean it in the English sense of being a place which contains drinking water, or the French sense of 'bien' relating to health and being?

She laughs. Waves of laughter from Morgana le Fay the sea born. Infectious, if she had not been dangerous. I have often thought, over the centuries, that she was a far more difficult opponent than Sir Bruce.

They are all worried about you.

I notice she does not say 'we'. I push my chair back to make room at the little table. She is wearing a thin summer dress. Teal. Little heart-shaped white buttons. Her long limbs are tanned. Her waist-length black hair flows with power over her body like the Gulf Stream. She sits, dress pulled up over her knees, legs apart. Unseemly. Handsome rather than pretty. Yet sexual. Very. She has often drowned men who have tried to plunge into her depths.

Are you still whining about a woman?

That was clever. By saying 'a' woman she avoided insulting Gwenevere. Avoided my wrath.

Which man of heart does not have a woman to whine about?

God, you were always so wet. I saw right through you. You know that.

I do. I did. I'm that I'm.

She frowned. *Now you're talking shite again. An avoidance tactic, M says.*

I know that the fat Merlin says many things. I say nothing. Instead I turn the ring which I wear on the third finger of my right hand in the true French style. The inner spell which says that Love begets Love helps to ward off her power. It is the best – the only – thing that I have brought with me from the otherworld.

Oh come on, stop taking the piss. That didn't work the first time remember? In Hereford? After your first escape and evasion?

I know of no castle, no battles up there. It must have been some other knight. She had known many.

I broke you remember? Remember the hoodwink? The white noise? Stark naked against a wall, babbling. Mine was the first face you saw when they removed it. Can't blame you for falling in love with me. Lots did.

I drink my tea. The cup rattles against the thin saucer. Too much traffic beyond. Too much sugar also.

The second time though – oh you were good. You had this blissful look on your face for 36 hours. It was all a game to you by that time. What a stiffy! Made me horny.

The waitress comes up. Nervously. I pay her well and she smiles. It is a huge smile. She folds the bundle of notes and conceals them from her boss.

You're still a sucker for a pretty face eh, 'Mr Dulux'? Hah! That'll be the ruin of you again.

Nimué taught me that I cannot be destroyed by giving: I can go to ruin by too much holding on. A gift given cheerfully has twice the merit. One which is given reluctantly brings no return. No one was ever destroyed by largesse, but many have been ruined by avarice. No point in trying to tell Morgana any of that. The wisdoms of the Sea are different to those of the Lake.

Yet Morgana's words trouble me as they always did. White noise? Hoodwink? Is it the faery song she means? And the falconry? These must have happened when I went to the place she had called the Val sans Retour. The Valley of No Return. 'Once you're in, you can never get out' she bragged. She trapped unfaithful people there. I, du Lac, broke her spell. I got out. She has never forgiven me. How? I admit, some things have slipped from my mind. I have lived too long in the Human world.

You went mad because of that little woman who obsessed you. Insane. You know that don't you?

There is no shame in that. Every text every written about Arser describes the madness of Lancelot. And of Merlin also. Arser was continuously mad but no-one dared say. I shrug, I smile, I look out of the window for hints of white shadow among the rooftops.

That smile... Exactly what you did on your second selection! Worked a treat, big boy. You thought you were fucking immortal didn't you? But I warn you that your little Jungian pal McHaffee has got one week. God help him.

I make my way downstairs. Behind me, waves of laughter.

You might need a mop up there, I tell the jolie little girl who is now grinning insanely after her very large tip.

I think it is Saturday. Evening. The bells have rung nine times so it is certainly after Compline. I am strolling in the town centre and have to tell the unalive ones to allez. Gently. I now understand their fascination for me. They have been waiting for a Champion for a very long time. It is not me, unhappily. I wish they would wash their hair. As a soldier I worry about lice.

The night is warm. The events of the previous days float in my memory like shoals of tiny electric-blue fish. I could spend every moment down below, holding my breath, just reliving the Queen's kiss on my neck. The more I recall, the more it felt like tiny bubbles. Thrilling.

I catch a glimpse of my squire strutting down Westgate Street towards the setting sun. Since he has been under my protection, Kelvin has become more lurid in his dress sense. He has the power, now, to be Who he is. Perhaps. Yet his clothes are outré. Tight, skin-tight trousers and t-shirt, bright red. High black boots, with heels. Plus a strange little black jacket of the sort bullfighters might wear. He is wearing full make-up. I can see that even though he faces away from me. There are highlights in his hair. I must remind him again that he is a Squire, not a minstrel or jester.

I follow him. Using skills I have learned behind enemy lines. I become invisible. An atom. He comes up against a group of drunks before the Garrick's Head pub. They are eating burgers and swigging from cans of lager. I note with a sigh and tut-tut, that I would never see this in France.

They start chanting *Iron Hoof Iron Hoof Iron Hoof*. A term I am not familiar with. But I can sense from the reddening of Kelvin's face and the stiffening of his posture that it is not a compliment. To my delight, and no small surprise, I can see his whole spirit limbering up for combat. I stand in a shop doorway and spy, intrigued to see how much he may have learned.

Ah, oui, there are his feet in the correct position: weight on the left foot pointing forward, right foot transverse, forming a T. Perfect for resisting a frontal onslaught. His attitude, his aura is good. With my extraordinary vision I can see his War Face. Well, he will need to practice this one. More of a lop-sided simper than a life-threatening snarl. However – pourtant – he is young.

They are all some distance away. One hundred French feet perhaps. I can read their body languages with an ease that obviates the need to hear words. The Bad People, for all their noise and bluster, are scarcely literate in the language of war. At least Kelvin has learned the first letters of the alphabet. If he has remembered merely the ABC of what I have taught, they will get a shock. If necessary, I will step out and help. I will not let my squire be harmed. On oath.

They altercate. Arms wave. The supine ones stand up. Their faces are masks of hatred. Their badness shines through. How many? Quatre. Four. Kelvin still maintains his posture, his attitude. Bien! Très bien!

The most bellicose steps forward. His face is red, his head is shaven. He has a sneering confidence. I am selfish. I yearn to swap places with my squire but I cannot.

The oaf – let me call him that – puts the flat of his left hand on Kelvin's chest as if to push him. As I taught, Kelvin places his own left hand on that, presses it hard to keep it in place. The oaf looks bewildered. No pain. Yet.

Bow, Kelvin, bow I telepath.

Kelvin bows. The oaf is forced downward. Startled.

Finger, Kelvin, finger I whisper on the wind of combat.

With a great HAH! my delightful squire, remembering all the bullies he has ever known, uses his right hand to snap his attacker's little finger.

Houp-là! I shout inwardly. Exultant.

The rest of the Bad People move forward. Uncertainly. I am ready to have some small amusement but to my surprise Kelvin is suddenly surrounded by the unalive ones. The crusties. They know he is connected with me. They want to help. To seek value and redemption via their Dulux. Even their dogs want to help. The Bad People get on their mobile phones. They call an ambulance. Why I do not know. It is only a broken finger, he can still walk, even if he is crying too much to talk. Kelvin is standing on the edge of the chaos, smug as Lucifer.

I feel it is time to teach him the D E and F when I see him next.

Well done my handsome prince says a voice. I feel another faery kiss but on the other side of my neck this time. It takes me by surprise. I forget to look out of the corner of my eyes and be still. I turn, startled, but Gwenevere is gone.

I know she is pleased. I go back to my apartement. I glow. I am sure my own shadows are turning whiter.

I will tell you about the Merlin. A little. So much I do not know. So much that is secret. Secrets flow through their veins in the same way that blood flows through ours. They swim in their secrecy as I swim in lakes.

The Merlins are a breed apart. I am not sure if they are Human or Faery. Or a nameless, separate race again. Older perhaps. They seem to pass their powers on like popes. They are always filled with plans and work to an agenda best known to themselves, sometimes doing evil to achieve some good. We can sometimes glimpse their actions and hazard guesses as to the bigger picture but they will never tell us all. They lie. Not constantly, but when they think necessary. That is to say, often.

I think there is one in every town. They have names like Hart, Stagg, Goater, Buck – all horned animals. They control the citizens in cunning ways although they would describe it as guiding them.

I was compelled to see one in Scotland. It was just after I had helped the Earl of Surrey defeat James IV of Scotland at the battle of Flodden. This must have been 1513, in human years. I think. I had no real stomach for the cause but I had made my oath to Arser, centuries before, so fight I did. With my guidance a small English force crushed one ten times as big.

The King of Scots lay there supine but alive. I bent over him. We lifted our visors together. *Ach, it's du Lac!* he said. *Yer no gonna stick me wi' that brown bill are ye?* The Brown Bill was something I had invented. It could rip apart armour like a can opener. I saw in his eyes that he was one of the Eternals like Le Comte de St Germain and Ahasuerus. Once the English had clearly won I used the confusion to help His Majesty from the battlefield. I liked him.

We spoke again 500 years later, at Third Ypres, when he took the name of humble Private Jimmy Forth. He told me that he had learned things from the husband and wife alchemists Nicolas and Perenelle Flamel, who had come to his court. I knew the pair well. A sweet little minx was Perenelle. Poor Nicolas regretted ever giving her the Elixir of Life.

As we parted company that day after Flodden, Royal Jamie told me, in excellent French, pointing over the Border hills:

Find the tower next to the lake. Find the little bird. Perhaps he can heal and help you. God bless you du Lac. May you find your shining lady.

He had deep insight did Jimmy. A great ladies' man. I think he wrought the secret of Eternal Life from Perenelle between the sheets while her skinny, intense husband was playing with his athanor. When he mentioned the 'little bird' I knew he was using the language of the Adept. He meant the small dark falcon known as the merlin.

I found the lake – of course! – I found the tower. A round tower – I am not allowed to say where. The Merlin was waiting for me. Dark, yes, but very large. Shaggy black hair, bushy beard. No fool. He had a great wolf-like dog with high pointy ears which he called Shuck. It went off into the woods as I approached.

The tower itself was unusual. Every one I had seen so far had their staircases going up the walls in a clockwise direction. Why? Because this gives the defenders the advantage on the stairs when wielding their swords. The Merlin's staircase, in stone, went the other way. He saw my look. My curiosity. He smiled.

It's because I'm left-handed.

We soldiers appreciate little details like this.

Sit laddy, he told me. *I ken fine yer worries.*

It was a fine round tower. Old rushes on the floor. High windows. Every neuk and cranny filled with large spiders and their webs. In the life he lived, and the plots he spun, he was one also.

Drink he said, giving me something like whisky in the hollow horn of a cow. It flowed through me, a powerful current through the centre of du Lac, overpowering and smoothing out the million eddies and whirlpools which had been tormenting my thoughts.

He lit two candles, beeswax. Brought out two wondrous mirrors that must have been made in a far country long ago. The finest I had ever seen. Standing behind me, stinking, his large gut pressing against my upper spine, he held the mirrors level with my face. One at each side. Angled.

Whaddye see?

It made me gasp. I saw a hundred images of du Lac, one inside the other. Diminishing into infinity.

Each one of ye. They are all real. They all exist the noo. Each mad bastard in there has his ain life, his ain destiny. They differ.

We all looked at each other. I felt kinship in the glass. Sorrow, but also support.

Yon bastard, three frae the left…he is in love wi' a Queen an' marries her. The ither, four frae the right, hates the Queen an rides off wi' her husband.

I was breathing heavily. The mirror on my right misted up. He had made his point.

They call me Lancelot I said, feeling I should introduce myself. *It is not a name I like. I am du Lac. When I perform bold deeds for the Good People I am the great du Lac.*

He shrugged, farted, then polished the mirrors on his sleeves before wrapping them in samite, fastening them with a red ribbon and storing them in a cupboard. He was not impressed. Greater men than me had come and gone.

They call me the Fat Pig mostly. Naebody knows ma role unless they have need. Few have need. Or… so… they… think he added, bending toward me and tapping his nose. Conspiratorial.

I came to learn that they all have their own skills. This one claimed 'To see the past that is to come. And the future that has gone before.' I did not understand. He did not want me to. Perhaps. Yet he went on: 'In a world beyond this world, and the Time after the Times to Come, you will remember yourself. All things will be well, and all things will be well.'

There was something about this great bulk of a Merlin that was comforting. He was like a great big old sow offering up all sorts of nipples for an invisible brood to suck upon. I would have stayed longer in that tower but he sent me away. His final words were:

You were carefully selected. Elite. You serve the Queen. You are her champion. Who dares wins. Who. Dares. Wins. The truth will hit you like a winged dagger one day.

I knew most of that already: I was chosen by Nimué; I am the greatest knight in the world; I continue to serve Gwenevere; I am still her champion; I have never lost because I have always dared.

I am still trying to fathom what I learned from that visit.

It is Sunday today. I can hear the bells from the Catholic church almost next door, calling to the faithful, but not to me. The fingers of sound tap against the outside walls. I am in a small white room that is not my own. There is much writing on the walls. Obscene. A few stick drawings that are execrable. It has a hard bed, a simple toilet and no windows. It is in fact a prison cell. I lie like one of the stone knights on the old tombs, one foot crossed over the other. I am comfortable enough. I am a soldier used to far worse.

The policemen came to my apartement last night. They arrested me with some embarassment and much *politesse*. One of them was the man I had taught skills to on the station platform. Godfrey, by name. He assured me they meant no harm. I had not thought otherwise. A gang had broken into Beckford's Tower and wrecked the place. The crusties must have poured in after Kelvin and I had left.

I was not of that gang I told him with absolute truth.

I know you weren't sir. But please come along with us.

They put me in a cell. It is almost jolie. After my sufferings in Castle Dolorous everything since has been jolie. Almost. I started a game of chess in my head to help me sleep. I slept.

Now, Sunday, there is a fury of things being done to bolts and locks. The door opens with a slight hiss.

Doctor McHaffee to see you sir, said Godfrey.

The man comes into my cell waving a clutch of paperbacks in each hand as if they are wads of money.

I've got these from your flat. You've read all of them and dog-eared certain highly-significant pages. You are all in here. I've got you now.

I was intrigued. Flattered. He kept running his fingers through his hair as he sat on the edge of the cot. Certain sign of fear. Had Harris and Dunne visited him again? Threatened again? My enemy's enemies would be my friends.

You're a lying con says the visitor. I use the French word as I tell you this. It is less vulgar. *You deny that you believe you're Lancelot yet you call yourself du Lac and seemed amused to be called Dulux by your little gang of scruffs.*

I play the chess again, but in my head. Then he came at me, full gallop, words out front as stiff as a lance. Yet I had not even donned my armour or mounted. The coward. The lunatic.

It is all in here. 'Lancelot of the Lake' by Anon. I've got you now. You've read this whole book and somehow transferred your own experiences and torments – whatever they are – into the stories. I must admit that as a die-hard Jungian I find it rather appealing. I quite like the thought of being a figure in your parallel Arthurian realm.

This guy, this Lancelot – you – only learns his own name on a tombstone after he has rescued Arthur and Gwenevere for the first time. Hence your pissy denials about the name Lancelot and your assumed identity. He – like you – is of mixed race. The author goes on about it for nearly three pages. He – like you – has mysterious 'absences', almost like what they used to call petit mals.

He holds the book toward me, his middle finger with bitten nail holding it open. I have already told you about my dual heritage. I had no intention of saying anything to this madman.

Is it your father who is Afro-Caribbean or your mother? Were you brought up in care? Do you think of the army as your family? Our Queen Elizabeth as some sort of proxy mother-figure?

I smile. It infuriates him. I look down at the cinema-screen before my heart and reminisce: my father was Faery, my mother Human. I was brought up in care by the Lady of the Lake. Simple.

Everything about you cries out that you're ex-military, probably ex-Special Forces. A complete outsider with PTSD. Trained to kill without remorse. Trained to resist interrogation. SAS? MI5? MI6?

I lie back on my cot. Push him off the edge with my laceless boots. He jumps up and stands nervously in the corner wondering what manner of being I am.

I think you did something bad. Really bad. Something you can't forgive yourself for. I think you need to strap on armour – the whole White Knight thing. I think you pushed yourself into this Lancelot archetype to get some support.

He looks into another book. It is called The Quest of the Holy Grail. He waves that before me too. He holds two of them, open, at either side of my face. Eerily like the fat Merlin had done with the mirrors, centuries before.

3 knights won the Holy Grail: Galahad, Perceval and Bors. All virgins. You had to be a virgin to get anywhere in Camelot. Whereas you had to – oh! OH! You're driving me into it aren't you? I'm getting sucked into your own story. I'll start again: **Lancelot** *had to look on enviously through the window. He was denied the Grail because of his affair with the Queen. He stood there wondering if his love for Gwenevere was worth it.*

There was no question. The Grail was a trick. It was candy floss for children: big, fluffy, sumptuous, wickedly tasteful, but with no substance, and dissolving in moments, leaving behind a useless stick. I, du Lac, was looking into their holy room feeling sorry for the prancing poofs inside. They were surrounded by lithe, gorgeous other-worldly women and they did nothing. Waste waste waste. Galahad was such a idiot. If he was my son, as Elaine kept saying then… then… No he could not have been. Never. Jamais.

What time is it? I ask.

He looks up. Looks at his watch. It is a cheap watch.

11.10.

Morning or evening?

Morning of course.

Then it is time for me to go, I tell him. Briskly. I sit up. I stand up. He huddles back into the corner near the door as if I might be about to attack him. In truth, vraiment, I was a little disappointed. Sir Bruce san Pitié has clearly lost some of his power since he has taken up Compassion as a business. I see the digit move on his watch: 11.11.

The door opens. Young Godfrey comes in, along with Kelvin. The former returns my laces. Kelvin, somewhat prickly in the presence of his former employer bends down and laces my boots for me.

But he's under arrest! says Sir Bruce to the policeman.

We're letting him go. The CCTV showed nothing more than these two wandering around the rooms, doing no harm, touching nothing. They'll get a fine in due course. All the damage was done by those who broke in later. Some of them are still there, squatting.

Kelvin helps me into my jacket. Makes a great show of dusting it down and straightening the wrinkles. He dissembles well before Sir Bruce. He is smug as Satan this time.

These are mine I say, taking the books back and shoving them into my deep white pockets.

*You **are** protected you bastard. Aren't you?*

Of course I was protected! Bien sûr. There has always been a small nucleus of people in each generation that know exactly Who I am, and have enabled things. I think it is probably the Merlins who oversee this. Whether out of anger or thanks because I ruined the original plans for Arser I am not sure. I must accept what they give me, and where they place me on their webs.

Who? He roars after me.

Of course, he means Who is protecting me but I choose to misunderstand. It is like a misericord into his ribs. I turn and reply.

Who? I am du Lac! I say, nodding and smiling at the very chic young policewomen who happen to be lining the corridor just then. *Enchanté, enchanté and enchanté* I say. One of them curtsied. I am sure I saw the faery gold in her eyes.

My squire and I went from the prison cell that morning to the nearby Parade Gardens that line the riverbank next to Pulteney Bridge. The air was full of sparkles. So was my heart. I could hear the first, most delicate notes of faery music. Oh she was very near. Gwenevere.

We took two striped deck chairs and sat overlooking the powerful rushing waters of the weir. A few young boys were jumping fully clothed from the levels above in a dare that Kelvin told me is called tombstoning. I counted them as they disappeared under the waters, ready to stride in, along the river bottom, to help them if necessary. It was not necessary. They all re-emerged, shivering but happy. There were pleasure boats on the other side of the River Avon taking on board tourists. Smaller craft that people seemed to live upon full time, with chimneys that smoked. In the Victorian bandstand to our right a local orchestra was blasting out summery tunes. Small children played in the lush grasses watched over by happy, relaxed parents. I had fought hard all my long life so that Britons could have the freedom to be like this. Even the people here in Gorre.

So who are you? Really.

Kelvin looked at me over the top of his ice cream cone. There was a teasing tone in his voice.

I am du Lac. Truly. Vraiment

Why did you walk over this weir naked?

It amused me that Kelvin saw this as a large weir.

It is not a weir. Not to du Lac. To me it is a Sword Bridge.

He looked puzzled, so I told him a story as the fat Merlin might have done.

There was a knight who made haste to rescue his lady, I told him. The only way to get there quickly was by crossing the narrow bridge made of a single, long sword blade. As long as three lances. Narrow. Sharper than a scythe. Stretching above and across swift and dark raging waters. He removed the armour from his feet and hands. He knew he would be in a sorry state when he reached the other side, for he would have to support himself with his bare hands and feet upon the sword. Yet he felt no fear of such wounds; he preferred to maim himself rather than to fall from the bridge and fail his Lady. He thought upon his Queen and passed over with great pain and agony, being lacerated in the hands, knees, and feet. But even this suffering is sweet to him: for Love, who conducts and leads him on, assuages and relieves the pain.

Kelvin looked impressed. Disbelieving but impressed. He stared down toward the weir which, even in the warmth of a summer's day, looked menacing.

So you did this for some woman? Proving your worth?

Extending my worth. Not proving it. Yes.

So where is she?

Somewhere in this kingdom I whispered.

Actuellement, there was no need to whisper. I had come here with Kelvin in case Sir Bruce or even the police had planted listening devices. The sound of the river protected us from such intrusion. I wanted to talk to my erstwhile companion knowing that he would pass on certain mis-information to Sir Bruce. Kelvin might be my squire but there are ways in which I might use him.

Okay Okay. Sir. You're du Lac. There's no evidence that King Arthur ever existed.

Bien sûr! He was always hiding from your scholars in plain sight. Historically he was... ah zut, but you must find him for yourself! Yet he was also more than just an historical figure. As you are more than Squire Kelvin. He was – still is to some – oh... what is the term in English? Ah. Oui – a bright shining hope. I was drawn to him like a moth to the flame. We all were.

Kelvin licked around the ice cream in his cone, turning it into a pure hemi-sphere. He was so like a child. Enwrapped in the moment. Unaware that we were being watched.

So let me get it straight. You, du Lac, joined King Arthur's court. What year was this?

Well, according to one of the chroniclers, it must have been about the year 450 but I think it is also last year. Or the year before – perhaps. Time for du Lac is like a fountain: it flows, ever-becoming.

You're a fucking nutter you are. Sir!

He said it fondly. I took it in that spirit. Though I did knock his ice cream from his hand as a token rebuke. He laughed. It was almost a faery laugh.

Then you fell in love with Gwenevere.

I was in love with both.

Oh! You tart! he exclaimed, imagining sexual dilemmas. Hoping for himself and me? Perhaps.

And Merlin? What about him?

No-one knows about the Merlin. He engineered King Arser's very existence. He brought Gwenevere into this world also. He had mighty plans. I ruined them.

Or rather the forget-me-not did. I chose not to mention or explain that. How can such power be contained in such a fragile stem? How can anyone else understand? I was foolish. Certainly. Yet my foster-mother the Lady of the Lake once told me: 'The sins of this world cannot be committed without folly, but one has good cause for folly if one finds reason and honour in it. And if you find folly in your love, that folly is glorious above all others, for you love the pinnacle and the flower of the whole world.'

A fleeting shadow crossed my brow as it often did when I thought about Nimué. Either a bird or a might-have-been. Or the slight suspicion that she often talked – as the English would say – bollocks, and had manipulated me as ruthlessly as Merlin had done young Arser. I had an uncomfortable feeling then. Had I seen Merlin recently – in human terms? Or was it long ago? Was he still trying to manipulate the world and me?

Enough history for now, Squire.

He shrugged.

I broke someone's little finger a coupla nights ago. Just like you taught me.

Did he deserve it? I asked innocently, not wanting him to know that I had been in the background, ready to help.

He was one of the Bad People he replied. Smiling.

I nodded my approval.

Eh bien. Now stop talking. Sniff. Smell. What do you smell?

Erm... you really are weird. Sir. But since you ask... Grass. River water. Cigarette smoke from that woman passing by. The faint odour of steak from one of the restaurants. Fart – that was me, sorry. And your aftershave. Joop, I think it is.

Below. Smell below all these.

He bent his head as if putting it under water.

What? What?

Gun oil.

What!?

From a SIG Sauer P226 Semi-automatic pistol.

Crap.

Two actually.

Two craps?

Two pistols. Concealed. Inside the jackets of those men behind us.

When I fought my way through the shattered streets of Caen in 1944 I gained a reputation. Supernatural. Almost. I could tell exactly where the Germans lurked. Invisible to everyone else who merely used their eyes, I du Lac used my nose. I could smell the different gun-oil they used to lubricate their excellent Schmeisser sub-machine guns. So different to that used by the British for their primitive but no less effective Sten guns. Then there were the cigarettes: the Ecksteins, Junos and Mokris which I could scent a hundred British yards away and smelled so different to the Lucky Strikes and Woodbines favoured by the Allies. And then, et puis, because the German diet was so very different too, I could tell from the faeces that they had been in a building, and when. I am not sure my mothers would have been proud of these skills but they saved many lives. No need to tell Kelvin any of this yet. He would only believe me through experience. I whispered:

Do not turn and look.

He turned and looked. Said they looked like Mormons. Admired their suits on a hot day. And haircuts. Suggested I might be paranoid. I gathered my wits. These must be the men Sir Bruce described as Harris and Dunne. Solicitors? Assassins. He was not convinced.

Why them? Because they look like Men in Black? Why not that crustie sitting cross-legged under the tree over there, staring right at you?

He meant the one I had come to call The Wild Man: festooned with facial piercings. The one I had first seen in Union Passage – or was it Green Street? And then again at Beckford's Tower. Or was it at the tower known as Brown's Folly? The underwater currents in my mind's lake are very strong at the moment. They knock me askew.

Squire Kelvin… I want you to pick up that melting ice cream from the grass. Make a great display of disgust on your way to that waste-bin between those two Bad People.

And then?

And then, et puis, stick it in the nearest guy's left ear.

His laugh was a loud bray this time, like the mules used to make in Flanders when the cannons started. Most unfaery-like.

Yah? That's ridiculous. Reeeediculous!

He is wearing a communication device in his ear. He is in contact with even badder souls than himself.

It's a hearing aid for Christ's sake. I think…

It is not.

He was laughing, bent double in the deck chair. He would learn.

So if I did, what then?

Then I will disappear.

If they are agents, they'll beat the shit out of me.

Do not, do NOT attempt to fight them. Even with your new skills. They are dangerous men. They know you are a dupe, harmless.

Oh thanks. Sir!

As soon as they see I am gone they will leave you and try to follow me.

The sun was warm. It was a perfect day. Still Sunday, I think. With my all-encompassing vision I could see Harris turning the pages of what purported to be a Bible, while Dunne pretended to read the Church Times. Kelvin looked at them and he looked at me.

You. Are. A. Nutter. God I love you for it, I really do, but I am not –

He stopped in mid-sentence. Although as a Frenchman I love Cartesian logic, I also understand the persuasive powers of the crisp £20 notes that I waved in front of his English face.

Okay. Yah, but what if they are just Mormons?

Then say you are sorry, that you know not what you do. And they will forgive you. Certainly.

He found it amusing. I like it that my squ
of danger. He got himself out of the deck chai
loud tutting noises at the messy confection. P
with distasteful grimaces – perhaps too man
wastebin holding it at arms length, dripping, li
in the Holy Grail farce. And then – et puis – di

I moved, with supernatural speed. Harris
chance of following.

As an old soldier I have great need of maps. Detailed. They speak
to me. When I left Kelvin to deal with the Bad People I leapt on my
destrier and visited all the likely parks, looking for the sort of ironic
clues and puzzles that Gwenevere is always likely to set me. Then I
saw, in tiny letters, a cluster of woods on the southern rim of Bath
called the Fairy Wood, which seemed to flow into the Rainbow Wood.
If my lady was to appear anywhere it had to be in one of those places!

I set spurs to my powerful mount and roared across town,
parking next to an old toilet block and striking – with silent skills
– into the trees. I am now lying on my back in a circular clearing
within the Fairy Woods. The trees reach upward around me like
eyelashes. Gwenevere often told me how she loved and envied my
own long eyelashes, so I am comforted. I have been here for some
time and glimpsed nothing. Yet. Small creatures, courting couples,
abandoned rubbish.

Now I am – what is the English word? – reminiscing. For me, this
is like lying in a warm pool at dusk. There is still an hour of daylight
left. Less. The sun comes through the branches and leaves of the tall
thin trees like a million silver arms, each one caressing me. Each one
creating a wavelet of remembrance like song. It must be how babies
feel in the womb. Peaceful. Safe. Timeless. Far above me, in a sky as
indigo as the depths of my lake, white birds swim across in hectic
paths, like brief memories.

Does water have memory? I, du Lac, say it does! Once, I was
having café au lait with a French scientist whom I had rescued from
some Parisian thugs. In Professeur Benveniste's laboratory, using
only droplets of water, a simple forgot-me-not, and a powerful
microscope, I was able to show him that pure water could somehow

what it had previously contained. I do not understand the s. I know the poetry is exact.

He looked up from the microscope. All he had previously understood, or believed, was being flooded by revelation.

If this is so, mon ami, then oceans and rivers and rains might be transporting all manner of information throughout the world.

Dare to believe. Somehow, the Lady of the Lake uses this occult and entirely natural 'science' to travel where she wills. I cannot explain, I have said all I know.

Un moment said the professeur, whose excitement was rising like a rip tide. *Give me a glob of your spittle. Please?*

He put it on a slide. Put the slide under the microscope. Put his eye to the eye-piece. Straightened with shock. Bent and looked again. Straightened with even greater shock. Stared at me. It looked as if he might be about to make the Sign of the Cross.

Mon dieu… he whispered. *You must be…*

But du Lac was already flowing out of his life forever.

Sign of the Cross? Another splash of reminiscence. J'aime remémorer!

It was rumoured among the fées that Gwenevere came into the Human world on a mission. Connected, somehow, to The Man Jesus and the True Arthur. As if the latter was a mystic reflection of the former. It seemed to me, growing up 'in the lake', that half the faery kind believed Jesus to have the white blood of the fées in him. That he existed as much in our realm as he did the Human. He is one of us, they would insist. No-one ever said that of me. Not in either of the worlds.

Zut, the whole Jesus thing meant nothing to me. I was a young man. I was learning how to fight and be the best knight in all the worlds. In some ways The Man Jesus (for I cannot think of him as anything more than a man) came between us as much as Arser.

Above me the stars are starting to peek between the highest branches. The breeze upon the leaves is like gently rushing water. I am relaxed and looking out of the corner of my eyes as always, looking for the fées to swim up through the aethers and come nibbling at me. Bringing me news. There is motion among the shadows and many presences, but shy and hesitant. Afraid to come forth. Typical of so many fées these days. The earth beneath feels hollow. As if I am lying on a thin crust that might easily break and send me tumbling down. A single blade of grass is blown against my cheek, tickling. I wish it might have been Gwenevere, and remember the times in the forests of Logres when she did exactly that.

I, du Lac, who have only ever known one love but for an exceedingly long time, am aware of the trivial acts that can trigger love among the Humans. I have seen a million such: a smile, a thank you, simple gifts and light touches, kind deeds or words. Simple acts enable floodgates to open so that Love can come surging through.

I look back at the other knights in the court of Camelot – in every court in all the kingdoms – and marvel that they scythed through the adoring damsels like they were ears of corn, nothing caring for the future, nothing caring for their hearts.

I never did as they did. My heart of wax was so firmly moulded toward one person only that it might as well have been diamond. Yet if it had not been for a single act, at a crucial moment, I might well have resisted her glamour and kept true to the King. What was the single act? It was she who first buckled on my sword at the court, in the absence of the King. So, technically, it was *she* who made me a knight, not Arser. To her it was just a passing action. To me it was High Magic. She was warm, pure, light, and smelt of summer. Her laugh was all the colours of the rainbow from lusty red to noble violet.

As I lie here in the grasses of the Fairy and Rainbow Woods, and watch the bats flitting in the dusky sky, and pretend that the passing traffic is the sound of the sea, I can summon up the whole moment. I am there. I have never left. It is pure. Purer than anything the virgin prig Galahad had ever known. What kind of Grail would choose him before me? And do not get me started about his 'friend', Peerless Perceval.

Had it not been for that act of Gwenevere fastening on my sword I might have had fun cutting a swathe through the women and siring many admired bastards. The fat Merlin insisted that was my right. 'There's not a wench here that doesn't want to swive with you.

They are gagging for it', he once whispered – or the Early Medieval equivalent of such words. I forget them now. In truth he had noticed the currents which were starting to flow between Gwenevere and me. He wanted to stop us. It was he – I am sure – who engineered my night with Elaine.

I lie here and shudder on the grass as I remember a moment of sex that damaged the world, and ruined me. Perhaps. I was given strong drink. Mead. In a filled horn that I could not put down. My first. Alcohol becomes wicked when it hits the faery bloodstream as you should know. Merlin and a couple of his lackeys carried me to my chamber. He whispered: 'In the next hour you must remain completely silent. There is a King next door. He would not be happy if he knew WHO is about to visit you.' He removed the candles from the room and sealed the windows so that the room was in utter darkness. I was too drunk to question this.

I assumed he meant that King Arthur was next door. I did not know that King Pelles was visiting with his daughter Elaine. When she came in and put her finger to my lips and mounted me and rode me like she rode her palfrey I did not question. I thought it was Gwenevere. I was drunk. I wondered, dimly, why her breasts were slightly larger but I enjoyed it. She left as silently as she had come. The next day, when I found out what had happened, Merlin denied that he had deceived me. 'I did not lie. You deceived yourself.' The whole court knew of that night. Gwenevere was furious. For a while. She made a great and public fuss of Arser to hurt me. It did.

I have not touched alcohol since.

I have not entirely trusted the fat Merlin since.

The sun gives a last flicker and it is night. Do I hear the chimes of Compline from somewhere? I might allow myself to drift off to sleep and sink into my own depths. I am sure the fées are watching from behind the trees. Shyly. They sometimes come to me in dreams. I have had many true encounters with Gwenevere in that way. Few of them satisfying. I lie spread-eagled like The Man Jesus. A small part of me wants to cry out: *Gwenevere, Gwenevere, why hast thou forsaken me?* But I know she has not. She is trapped, imprisoned. Near. Besides, my occasional bouts of self-pity used to annoy her. So

I fight with myself about this, and try to unhorse the Chevalier de Autopitié before he can even spur toward me.

An old poem comes to mind. By Thomas Macaulay whom I saved from footpads – or was it Mohocks? – on the streets of London. I cannot remember the year. I know Victoria was alive. At the time of the Great Stink. Perhaps. He took me back to his grand house to meet his friend Lord Lytton and later I spent a few evenings educating him into the diplomatic language of High French. I know he sensed Who I was – and am. I do not deny that I get a certain frisson when this happens. As if it justifies my long existence. On my last visit when we had finished our lesson he led me to the front door himself, snuffing out the candles as we went, and as I stood on the step almost chanted at me:

Those trees in whose dim shadow
The ghastly priest doth reign
The priest who slew the slayer,
And shall himself be slain

When he finished he slammed shut the great door. It frightened the pigeons off the roofs. Horses whinnied in the street as if from gun-shot. Behind it I heard locks and steel bolts being applied. The windows of the shutters were closed in unison by his servants.

Goodbye, I said to his life.

I want the words of that poem on my own tombstone. I think. They give me a dark comfort. A recognition. I say them out loud, but gently. Wistfully. I am indeed a ghastly priest. But of War in its nobler aspects? Or of Love in its bleakest?

As I lie here with such memories rippling over my mind I feel something licking my right palm! I peek out of the corner of my eye. At first I think it is a large dog but then it is outlined briefly by the high beams of distant passing lorry. I see the unmistakable form of a roebuck. Greeting me. A roebuck in the thicket. As Nimué once explained (well, a lot more than once), this is a symbol of the White Goddess. Whom we all should serve and once did.

I sit up. The creature seems to glow. It is otherworldly. It comes around and licks my other palm, and then each foot. The tongue is tiny, rough, it will leave scars. Bizarre. I look down at my chest, my heart, where my thoughts emerge. The colours of the forget-me-not are shining through my clothes. Illuminating the whole thicket. There are alchemies of light at work. The clumps, stumps and trunks of leaden blackness are beginning to glimmer, transmute into structures luminous.

I turn to my left. It is as though all the stars in the western sky are descending, coalescing, taking shape within the clearing in these mystic woods. There is a song within my blood, within every cell, which makes me want to cry. I cry. The tears are cool, silver, singing, the deepest water of my old heart.

Come home I hear Her voice say. It is a loving voice, in the tones of every mother who has ever been or will be. *You have done your duty to your king – and more. Come home. You will no longer be alone.*

What is Her name, this great Being who is rippling the stars of the Milky Way and brightening the darkness in my heart? I want to cry out *Maman!* But the ancient soldier in me feels this might be unseemly. I know this is She whom I visited as a child, at Lake Nemi. This is Diana of the Wood, for whom I was destined to be Rex Nemorensis.

I bow my head. I will bow to no man but I will bow to Her. I have only to reach out and I know that She will take me. Home. Into the peace. Yet I cannot. For it is not Gwenevere's voice I hear and I must find her first. My duty to the White Shadow must come even before the White Goddess. I took an oath.

It feels as if the whole heavens bend with her toward me. I cannot meet Her eyes, this goddess of the night sky and the Milky Way. I look toward the earth of the wood.

I summon up my words, carefully, lest I offend Her.

My Lady, I say, *I must –*

A hand grabs my shoulder. A very human hand. I turn.

Got you at last, says the Wild Man.

I, du Lac, am too strong to be startled, though I can occasionally be surprised. I did not expect to see that gaunt creature behind me with the fading goddess-light reflecting off his ugly facial piercings. Nor did I expect to see at least a dozen of the unalive ones standing silently behind him at the edges of the circular clearing. How had they sneaked up on me! On *me!* I am certainly getting too old.

I knew that She had gone. Seeped into the land like rain. The song in my heart had silenced also, and it felt that my rib-age was open to the sky. I made a gesture of closing it.

We faced each other, the Wild Man and I, like combatants. I felt no ire. No one can summon the Goddess if She does not want to come. No one can restrain or retain Her if her purpose is finished. Yet he radiated anger. It washed against my solidness like a small wave and flowed back to him. He glared. I swear I heard his piercings tinkle. If he had made an effort to attack me there were a hundred ways I could stop him. A thousand. With or without inflicting pain. Yet I did step back a centimetre when he said, softly, so that his gang could not hear:

Hello Dad. I think you've been avoiding me long enough. I find that rather upsetting.

What startled me was the contrast between his mien – one step up from a scarecrow – and his enunciation. All the cadences of the English boarding school and thus one of the High Born who are forever destined to rule in England. It was like that in Arser's time. It is like that now.

I brushed his pitiful slur upon my age in calling me Dad. Not too long before – was last week or last month? – Bad People had called me grandad before I thrashed them in rescuing that girl.

What do you want?

So many of his type were selling things or asking for money. Pitiful.

I just want you to acknowledge Who I am. That's all.

I understood him at once. It was like my arrival in Camelot. Nobody knew Who I was. I did not know myself. Did not even know my own name. Have I told you that?

You are a leader of the common people I told him, indicating the unalive ones standing expectantly behind him. Like a corrupted, Low Born version of the Round Table.

He frowned. Shook his head.

You know what I want to hear. Just tell me. What are you afraid of?

Nothing. Rien. Never. Jamais. So I spoke to him as if I really was his father:

Remove those trinkets in your face. Wash. Wear proper clothes. Get a job. Above all get a haircut.

He sighed. Took a deep breath.

What about my muh-

Before he could get out the word 'money' I pinched his mouth closed and held his lips shut. I might have given him something – all of them something – if he had not been so craven in his demand. It was unmanly. In fact I was about to give him an army-style dressing down, what the Tommies would call a bollocking, when the bizarre figure of Kelvin appeared.

Having fun? he asked, looking at the way I had the Wild Man muted. *Want me to break his finger?*

How did you find me?

I saw your bike parked next to the toilets. I knew you'd be clumping around in here somewhere.

I do not clump. And you look ridiculous.

He was clad in a one-piece suit of tight white leather. Too tight. It would restrict his movement in any fight. And the white helmet, like a spaceman.

Thank you! They were Mormons by the way. I've had some fun today.

They were not Mormons.

I looked at the Wild Man. He looked back at me with disgust. Some fear also.

Don't kill him said Kelvin. Teasingly.

The Wild Man's eyes widened. He tried to shake his head. The unalive ones behind him quivered in the night and started to fade away before they could start that stupid chant of Dulux.

Go I said quietly at first. And then *GO!* with a voice that echoed across all the seven hills of Bath. They went. I think the Wild Man started sobbing, pitifully, but he went too. Into the night.

It is Monday today. Evening. Certainement. I say this with some confidence because Kelvin has given me a small electronic calendar. It has large letters and numbers and has a curious green light that comes on at night.

He said I needed it because I am often 'away with the faeries' and never seemed to know where I am when I come around. There is some truth in this. The term is used with jocular (and sometimes scornful) intent today but when I fought for a King in Ireland the common folk saw this phrase as diagnostic. Some of those Celticky types would – through mind or spirit – cross over into faery, into the realm of the Shee. In the Human world they would be seen as almost dead. Entranced. Unmoving. When they came back, few would claim to remember what they did, or saw. Many, like myself, would wake to a great sadness.

I think it was like that glimpse the fat Merlin had given me of all the other du Lacs in the mirrors. Here am I in Bath, looking intently at my little calendar. One of the other du Lacs is walking softly through the golden meadows of Tir na nÓg – Land of the Ever Young. Perhaps our paths cross. Perhaps we coalesce briefly before moving on.

This little white time-telling device is clever. An ordinary watch or clock is too fast for my rate of being. I told you, seconds, minutes and hours mean nothing to me. I can cope with a display of days and months. Just. It is a love-gift of course. I am aware of Kelvin's feelings for me but I do not respond to his amours – I cannot! But nor do I take advantage.

I was ready for Sir Bruce when he came. I knew his arrival was imminent because someone left a large note for me on A4 paper saying DR MCHAFFEE @ 6.

The door behind me opened. I had no need to look around. I could hear him breathing heavily. Not from the many steps up to my apartement but from fear.

Pax he said. In an odd way. If a single syllable could be extended into three by a shaking voice, then it was that.

Pax.

He came before me and he was unshaven. There is no excuse for a man not to shave, except during times of extended combat. It was like a knight having rusty armour. It spoke of laziness and low standards. He kept looking out of the window to the street below.

Look, seeing as you won't engage with me, I'd like to you to do one thing. A simple Word Association test. I promise that I accept you exactly as who you say you are: this figure of du Lac. I will not try to challenge this or scorn it. I accept. Just do this one test and I promise that I will leave your life forever. Yes?

I nodded. Never had I seen Sir Bruce like this. Defeated before he had even begun.

As he paced back and forth between me and the window he threw the words at me like daggers. To me they were just words. He threw: Lake, Lady, King, Mother, Duty, Death, Army… I forget the others. Many others. Such tests show as much about their creators as they ever do about the patient/respondent. It was clear to me that Sir Bruce felt his own kingdom was falling apart. That he was being menaced by those who would take his crown and his very head. Strangers. He also seemed to have huge guilt.

My answers? They were simply words taken from the Sermon on the Mount, plus a few from the poem The Ancient Mariner, which we Eternals use as light comedy. We never quite finished the exercise, however, because I saw the Queen on the chessboard behind him moving by itself toward the edge, out of the pattern entirely. A very bad sign.

He started babbling:

We have physicists at the University doing research into wormholes and their potential for travelling through space and perhaps time, and here you are creating your route into the past using nothing more technical or mechanical than your guilt. What is your guilty secret? From where did your wormhole first begin?

I said nothing. Rien. What is more absurd: that I am a Bad Person who is racked by guilt, or that I am indeed du Lac, living on through the centuries racked by love?

Do you have sexual trauma of some sort?

Well, eh bien, the exercise stopped there because Kelvin came out of my bedroom clad only in my white dressing gown, the ample folds looking foolish on his skinny body.

Hi! he said to us both. Cheerily.

Oh said Sir Bruce. I could hear in that single word, and see in his sour expression, that he was making assumptions. I made no attempt to explain anything.

We stopped for a moment. Kelvin glowed at Sir Bruce. Sir Bruce looked worryingly at me and then at him. With my magical vision I could see them both at once, but my main concern was with that chess piece.

Look, both of you. I don't want to come here again. I won't. I don't care what happens to Tigh Aisling or the nutters I've collected. In five minutes' time I want nothing to do with either of you. I am out of my depth.

That he should make this confession to du Lac was filled with irony. Or do I mean poetry? Then he took a small device from his inside pocket to play some loud music. The tune was not familiar. It was not French. Oompahs featured loudly.

In case we're being bugged he whispered, summoning us to lean forward so that our heads were almost touching.

I know why you went mad. In the story of Lancelot he and Gawaine approach Gorre to save Gwenevere. They can only enter by two paths. One under the river, or the Sword Bridge over. Gawaine chose the former and failed. Lancelot chose the latter.

I raised my eyebrow in a powerful gesture.

*Because you once took a route **under** a river didn't you? And it all went wrong.*

This is getting good! said Kelvin, who shamefully tried to edge against me to upset his former employer.

First I want you to see this…

He took from his briefcase a small black laptop. His own version of the Little Book of Great Enchantment. Powered by batteries rather than dreams. His hands were shaking. Cowardice.

Kelvin sat on the white couch next to me. Crossed his legs. The little screen burst into life.

This is a documentary called 'The Murder of Princess Diana' Have you seen it?

Yah, said Kelvin. Nodding, enthralled.

I never watch television. I have enough channels in my own mind to occupy me.

He used one very agitated finger to make the pictures go forward. Fast. Then he paused them. Sir Bruce, who once wielded mighty lances twice the length of a tall man, now used a pitiful pencil to point at the image.

Here. Outside the hotel in Paris. Diana is leaving with Dodi Fayed.

The Saracen, I thought.

There. Look. Those two figures. Two men.

They were blurred. Grey.

The documentary maker says that these men are from rogue elements of British Military Intelligence. That one on the right… that's you.

Wow! burst out Kelvin. *Oh wow!*

He pushed me aside to get a better look. *It does look a bit like you. Same shoulders. Square head.*

My head is not square.

Wow! he said again, *You murdered Princess Di. That is so cool! They said that two guys in a Fiat Uno used a blinding light and remote control detonations on the brakes to make her car crash.*

Sir Bruce breathed heavily. In and out. In. Then he gave his final thrust:

Du Lux. Of the light.

Oh wow! They say she was pregnant by Dodi. That the Establishment didn't want a Muslim as heir to the Throne. It all makes sense. Dulux, Sir, this is amaaaazing!

I did something within me that was like putting my visor down. I glared at Sir Bruce through slits. I murdered no-one. I was angry with Sir Bruce for making this absurd suggestion. How could I, du Lac, a Priest of the goddess Diana do harm to a brave princess who bore Her name? Why would I, the greatest fighting man of all time, use such a crude technique even against a Saracen?

I could have killed Sir Bruce there and then with a single blow that would leave no marks. Dumped his useless body in the river. Been free of him. Forever.

I have met Jungians before. And their stupid word association tests which test nothing. He was using the distorted stories known as myths to create a fantastical realm of fantasy to explain me to himself. To excuse himself. The truth is so much simpler. Vraiment.

Sir Bruce was twitching my white curtains. Creating a narrow gap. Looking out of the window and down into the street again. Frightened of what he saw.

I might have taken him then but the Queen on the chess-board, already teetering, started its disastrous fall outside the pattern. I launched myself full length to catch it. Sir Bruce, thinking I was attacking him, gave the most unmanly yelp and bolted out of the room.

Kelvin remained. Looking at me adoringly. Impressed, no doubt, by my incredible reflexes.

Daft twat, he said.

If he is to continue as my squire I must modify his filthy tongue.

I am very tired today. I who am very old – ancient! – now start to feel it. For a fée, that is almost a death-knell. What is the poem? 'Age shall not weary them nor the years condemn'. Yes, that is it. Age is beginning to wear me now. Do the years condemn me? Not if you listen to the legends. Not now. Being chaste is no longer a spiritual requisite. However I, du Lac, condemn myself without pity. Increasingly I understand – yearn for – that world I came from yet never truly knew: The Land of the Ever Young. I remember the scenery with difficulty, as through the muddy waters of a deep and turbulent lake. Even so, I become homesick.

Understand me… I measure my existence in terms of monarchs and dynasties rather than years. I became *Who* I am under Arthur the Great. I suspect that I will come to my end during this reign of Elizabeth II whose life I have protected many times. Secretly. Or Charles III at the latest. And also, aussi, I confess that I have had great – what is the word in English? – perturbations, during the ebb and flow of the Stuart and Hanoverian dynasties and only found some peace within the House of Windsor. Always du Lac persists. I fulfil my Oath.

Did I tell you about when Arser was Arthur? What he was *really* like? Did I tell you that yesterday or last century? I think I did.

Arthur became old too, and then Arser appeared. When I – occasionally – look at the 'celebrities' of today and see how some of them use this 'plastic' surgery to maintain their smooth brows I think that this is a parallel. My golden king tried to keep himself young. Artificially. By style and pose. His great vision of the Two Worlds somehow turned plastic also. Something within him sagged but was pushed back into place. Then he got taken in by the scam of the Holy Grail that I must tell you about soon. In brief, he proved to be more Human than Fée.

No wonder Gwenevere turned to me. Plus I was a King's Son also. In fact, bien sûr, with my father dead I AM a king!

I am sitting amid the huge trees of the Circus, just along from Tigh Aisling on Brock Street. It is strangely familiar to me. Perhaps because it was built to re-create the grandeur of Ancient Rome. A circle of tall, Georgian Buildings penetrated by 3 roads, and a central grassy circle that has its own grove of massive trees. It is a structure that has no beginning and no end. Like me. The night is warm, even for England. The unalive ones are in the shadows. Their voices murmur like a rivulet. Knowing that I do not like dogs, they seem to have left them behind. Somewhere. I have no idea of where these people go when winter comes and the cold bites. But they are here now. They feel safe in my presence, though I am under no specific obligation to defend them.

The young policeman called Godfrey appears. He is an affable guy. If I did not already have a Squire I could do worse than him.

That was good work you did in Walcot Street, sir. But don't tell my Inspector I said that!

Thank you. I will not.

You put four thugs in hospital but nothing serious.

It was necessary. They were insulting a very young man in uniform. Who had taken an oath to serve.

He was a pizza delivery boy.

Does that matter?

His brow wrinkles as he ponders this for a moment. Then of course:

No. No it doesn't.

But he does an odd thing: he salutes me.

Do you need anything, sir?

I shake my head. I am fine. Bien. I ask him as an afterthought:

Do you need any more help fighting the Bad People tonight?

No sir. I think they're all in bed! They're afraid of this Dulux character. We've got half the nutters in Bath claiming to be him.

Everyone has a hint of du Lac within them. You more than others. Tell them to go away and become Who they are.

He frowns, thinking. I salute him back and he goes his lonely way. Although you understand, bien sûr, that I am saluting the uniform and the oath he took and what they both represent, and not the man himself. It is fitting that du Lac should be protecting a town with the name of Bath. Which is really a small, man-made lake for the purposes of hygiene.

No sooner had he gone than another person approached from behind. I could see with my extraordinary vision that it was a woman, plodding heavily across the grass. Holding something behind her back. A seraphic look on her face.

She is familiar. Where had I seen that shape before? That Mohican cut?

I remember. This is the lady whom the Bad People insulted on my first night in Bath. The one they called Miss Wibbly Wobbly.

I stand. It is only courtesy. She is a woman and therefore a Queen, despite her heavy army boots and ex-army jacket. She comes close. Looks up to me. She is shy.

Mr Dulux…

Enchanté.

Whatever she hides behind her back, she hesitates to show me.

What is it ma'mselle. S'il vous plâit?

She brings forward a string of white flowers, made into a chain, held carefully in her chubby fingers.

They're daisies. For you.

I am silent. Eventually I speak:

They are stars, ma cherie.

You're the bestest man I ever met. I tell ev'body.

What is your name, young woman?

Grace. I called Grace.

Then you have been named truly, wisely.

I bow. She has given me high praise, true praise, better than medals.

Grace puts the circlet on my head and I straighten. Without another word she turns and goes, boots clumping heavily when she gets to the pavement. Fading into the depths of the night.

Perhaps it is time to let go of my forget-me-nots…

The night is calm, the sky is clear. Gwenevere is somewhere within the orbit of these 7 hills. Very close. Yet there is a part of me which is troubled. I must say it now:

I have often thought, over the centuries, that I might have been used.

Did my foster mother the Lady of the Lake – who I suppose was actually my kidnapper – have her own plans for me? Was I, of noble blood, meant to supplant Arthur? Is that why she gave me my magic sword Seure, which she said meant Sequence? Was I just part of some sequence of kingship that she hoped to control?

Then Gwenevere… Did she just want me as a younger version of her husband, doing all the things with my body that he could no longer manage? She would never leave him. She had taken oaths of her own, in marriage and also – she said – through her plans for uniting the Two Worlds. Did she just love me for my royal blood? Would she have looked at me if I had been a commoner?

I must find the fat Merlin and ask him. Sometimes he lies, sometimes his truth is pure and simple – if hurtful. Sometimes his truths are from visions so far ahead that it takes the ordinary soul a little time to understand. Always, he bewilders. Controls.

It was on May 4th 1945 that I began to worry about these things. You might say with no little contempt that this took me long enough, but remember, s'il vous plaît, that I am a fée. Time is nothing. Or not much. And inside I am still this little lost, homesick boy. Innocent, trusting.

I was watching over the beaten German officers who had come to surrender. Unconditionally. There was Admiral Von Frieburg and General Kinzel and some lackeys. I was there because it was my duty to ensure that the war in Europe at least really was over, and that the kingdom was finally safe. My oath, you understand. My curse.

The upper ranks of the German officer class (filled with their remnant aristocracy), never dreamed that this mere private guarding them might be fluent in their language. Note well that as a warrior, the greatest fighting man of all time, it was always part of my weaponry that I became fluent in the tongues of my opponents. These men, despite being defeated and exhausted, yet had that air about them which reminded me of the Knights of the Round Table in their final days. Arrogant. Superior.

To a man, muttering among themselves before being summoned into Montgomery's presence, they blamed Corporal Hitler for their demise. They wished the various assassination attempts had succeeded, then they would have won the war without the Führer's inane and insane meddling.

Corporal Hitler.
The Little *Corporal*
That *Corporal.*

The word 'corporal' was said with complete scorn. It meant *scheisse* or shit the way they spoke: an emphasis of tone like a turd dropping into a bowl.

That was when my doubts began, there amid the rain atop a little tor on Luneberg Heath. An uncertainty I had not known since I had been a young man with Name Unknown. I had to suppress this, put my invisible visor down, because Montgomery summoned the generals to the meeting he had waited and prepared for all of his fighting life.

Good job private! he called to me. *Job done, job well done.*

He winked. I have often thought he knew exactly Who I was.

At the moment when the last German disappeared inside the tiny army tent I walked away from the Second World War. My job was done. Finis. For a time. I went into the nearby woods and sat down against a tree to think.

It was the fat Merlin who had said something to me once which I thought was innocent knowledge. Yet nothing that creature utters is innocent. He said:

Do you know who gave you this name 'Lancelot'?

Mais oui, it was my mother the Lady of the Lake. She had it inscribed on my tombstone when I was born.

We had some speculation as to what it might mean, as I think I told you. I thought it might be from *lancer l'eau*, and he made a crass joke about Big Dicks. Then he added, almost as an afterthought:

Do you know that it is actually from a very old word meaning 'Servant'?

I did not.

He laughed. He did that a lot. Using the technique of laughter and walking away to avoid a cross-examination he was able to imply a vast knowledge which could not possibly be shared.

I thought little of this comment then, being too deeply entwined with Gwenevere. Yet it came to me on that German heath like a slap on the face. Did the whole of Camelot see me as an eternal inferior, equivalent to this little corporal who had done so much damage to the world? Was I always seen as a mere servant of the Goodly Ones. Was that what Nimué intended me to be – a mere servant who would fulfil her plans? A servant of the Lake?

Merde and scheisse and shit.

Did I ever tell you about my madness? How being in love with Gwenevere and the True Arthur tore me apart? I will. Soon. I try to get through the pain by thinking of my White Shadow. When you are the greatest knight in the world, you are also the loneliest. I need to glimpse her again soon, or hear her voice. When this happens all such doubts fade and my love surges like a river bursting through a dam. But here, now, amid these high buildings in an alien town, at the ending of my world, clutching the little chess piece, I struggle.

I will tell you of our first night. Chrétien got it right. I have often wondered how he knew so exactly. I have the page here, torn from the book. Listen, ecoutez:

> *And the Queen extends her arms to him and, embracing him, presses him tightly against her bosom, drawing him into the bed beside her and showing him every possible satisfaction; her love and her heart go out to him. It is love that prompts her to treat him so; and if she feels great love for him, he feels a hundred thousand times as much for her. For there is no love at all in other hearts compared with what there is in his; in his heart love was so completely embodied that it was niggardly toward all other hearts. Now Lancelot possesses all he wants, when the Queen voluntarily seeks his company and love, and when he holds her in his arms, and she holds him in hers. Their sport is so agreeable and sweet, as they kiss and fondle each other, that in truth such a marvellous joy comes over them as was never heard or known.*

She loved me. Loves me. The whole of the Two Worlds must know that. But Chrétien knew – I do not know how – that the depth of my love, my intensity, was far greater than hers.

To be fair, the Merlin in one of his more human moments did try to console me:

Understand, du Lac, that she is pure fée. Pure. The fées are a collective. They are not individuals like humans are. That is one of the things they want to learn from us. You are half human, on your true mother's side. Gwenevere will never be able to give to you what you give to her.

So it is my Birth Mother's fault that I hurt so much. In truth, the older I get, the more I miss the woman that I never knew. She would see the boy within me, and make all things well with a simple cuddle.

And so I cling to the image of Gwenevere ever more strongly. A man cannot detach himself from his shadow – even a white one.

Yet my madness. You must know. There is no shame, these days, in such a condition. In this century they talk glibly about Post Traumatic Stress Disorder. A phrase which trips off the tongues of those who have never known combat, and their heads nod and they say: *Yes yes we understand* – while understanding nothing.

This PTSD is not what afflicted me then or now. Not the fighting, not the killing and relentless slaughter. If I might construct a term in my clumsy English it was Traumatic Love Stress Disorder that broke me. Chronic TLSD.

Then when Elaine appeared at court with the boy she said was my son, and Gwenevere was so hateful to her, and Elaine herself (fair and worthy I admit) showed clearly that she loved me as I loved Gwenevere, and then when I saw that the True Arthur had decayed into Arser and the whole Round Table was a bunch of sniggering poseurs... Sequence and consequence. Round and round.

Gwenevere's rage. Perhaps someone like the Merlin or Gawaine (second best knight in the world), or even the lady-loving Sir Bruce might have had the arguments which could fend, or the words that can stab a response, but I am a soldier. Gwenevere lashed me for my betrayal with Elaine. She loathed the boy called Galahad, and said he was ugly. That she was still married to Arser and had no intention of leaving him, because of her oath. As ever. Everything was always because of her oath.

She wanted my entire love, my soul and body, yet she blamed me for giving her them and bringing her so much grief.

She's jealous said Elaine, pushing the boy toward me, then trying to hug.

She took an oath, I responded. Weakly. I wonder what might have happened if Ahasuerus had asked me to consider – to pretend to imagine – that oaths were nothing more than wind? Would I have decayed as he did? Not unless Gwenevere decayed with me.

Nevertheless I left Camelot with Elaine and my bastard. We

started a new life together. She was happy. The boy was weird. I gave up exercise, gave up jousting. Refused to pass on my skills to the boy. Refused to use his name as I refuse to respond to Lancelot. If Love begets Love does Misery beget Misery? It surely does.

Gawaine, one of the Good Ones, tried to help me:

Friend, friend… Elaine is truly lovely. She is a King's Daughter. She is not just fair, she is utterly beautiful and kind. She adores you. Can you not find happiness with her?

Have you ever loved anyone as I love Gwenevere?

He pondered. He sighed.

No-one can love that much.

So I tried to become someone else. Someone ordinary. I lost weight. Rarely slept. Had no interest in Elaine as a woman. Went for long walks, ignored the horses. Slept a lot, hoping to dream of my Queen. Sometimes I did.

I knew that the moment Gwenevere snapped her fingers I would come running. She did so. Her maids brought secret messages. Everyone knew. We met in glades, caves, hidden bowers. Secretly at first, deceiving Elaine completely. I thought. In truth she loved me so much, wanted and needed me so dreadfully, that she put up with my perfidy. Who does that remind you of? Me? The True Arthur?

I broke.

No longer was I the great du Lac, finest knight in the world. I was a small puddle. Evaporating.

And then, et puis, there was the Holy Grail. That was almost too much. Listen, I will tell you quickly.

The Merlin knew that Camelot had become effete. Too many pretty, self-admiring young men striving for advancement. The Round Table had become more like a bunch of Civil Servants talking about their gold-plated pensions. So he set up challenges for various knights to try and hone their skills and maintain their hunger but they tended to fall flat. Read your Malory if you want details.

That was when the Holy Grail 'appeared'. You can tell from my tone I always felt it was something arranged by the fat guy. Probably.

I will be honest. Although I have compared it to a modern dish made of Tupperware that is just my spleen. I really do not know what it was. Or is. Or if it even existed without the strange potions that the Merlin would offer to his chosen ones.

I just recall looking into a candlelit room where a lot of comely young ladies marched around with a long spear – a lance!? – dripping into a bowl while my 'son' Galahad and his very best friend Perceval seemed to be drooling down their white tunics. But not, alas, at the women.

I tried to enter, to save them from their folly. To slap them gently and tell them to come back into the world and be manly. I tried to tell them to learn about love and their two hearts of wax and diamond and not get drawn into Arser and the Merlin's play-acting.

Something stopped me. Knocked me unconscious. I do not know what. A great voice? A bolt of lightning striking my armour? God?

When I woke the two maiden boys and their maiden spear-carriers had gone. As if they had never existed. Never to be seen again. The room was empty, just curtains blowing. It stank of rotting fish. The court adjoining was full of wide-eyed idiots and Arser was telling people that it was all downhill for Camelot from now on.

Why not me? I asked the wobbling and very smug Merlin when he was snuffing out the candles.

Because you aren't chaste.

Merde. If chastity and purity and being high born is what the Humans need to enter their Heaven and meet their Jesus, I want nothing of it. Yet I am remembered today not for my courage, or my sense of duty, or my sacrifices, but because I was not chaste when a bunch of arseholes seemed to think it mattered.

I am not sure if it was that day or centuries later but I recall the Merlin telling me that I was pure BS. As a soldier that only means to me Bullshitter. I grabbed his shirt and glared. Suggested extreme violence through my fierce eyes. Yet he had the trick of making offensive comments and then backtracking to imply that he meant something flattering, if only we were smart enough to understand. He did this then:

No, no you daft sod. I mean you're a weird kind of faery BodhiSattva.

You put off entering Paradise until everyone else is safe and can enter with you.

I pushed him away. His words meant nothing. They still do not.

It is Thursday morning. Terce. I spent an hour at Matins in an empty playing field in a part of Bath known as Combe Down. Not far from the Fairy Wood. I was furious, but have calmed down since.

Whenever I have had a sleepless night and get too distraught I rise at dawn, face the sun, and have an imaginary battle with Sir Bruce. Were you to watch me – and many have – you would see a strong, handsome man waving a sword which is invisible to onlookers but all too apparent to me. In my mind's eye I summon up Sir Bruce's wretched image and slice, thrust, parry and slash. I stab and chop, spin and cut. I jab and impale. I use all those talents for poise and balance that once got me invited to join the Ballet Russe.

The man called McHaffee would have deemed me mad. Squire Kelvin would have laughed and called me (with his English affection) a nutter. The good citizens of Combe Down – or at least a dozen of them – looked on with delight, and asked whether Tai Chi sessions were going to be offered at their village hall.

Why was my night sleepless? First, because Morgana had slipped into the covers beside me and after some cold, almost serpentine sex had warned me that camera crews from the local news station were trying to track down this Dulux character. That he was becoming as much a cult figure as some street artist called Banksy, with no-one quite knowing who he was or where he would strike next. Then she told me that Dr McHaffee – her term, not mine – had written a most unsatisfactory report.

This is all becoming too public for M. You know what happens next, don't you?

When it comes to the Merlin, I never know what happens next. I am a soldier, not a philosopher. I told her to go. After brushing my feet with her long, black hair and calling me a charmer and a maniac and the best she had ever had, she went. Retreating with a kind of murmur, like the sea after high tide. For someone as deep as she, sorrow seemed to fleck across her features in breaking wavelets.

Of course, I then had to see what had been written about me and broke into the Doctor without Medicine's offices in a sad little back street in Combe Down.

It was easy to break down the office door. I knew he would not be there. The place was filthy. As a soldier I know that it is necessary to keep your living quarters and your working places as neat and tidy as your own self. It requires effort, an eye for dirt, and determination to let your outer world reflect your inner. Otherwise you get lice, trench foot, and all manner of avoidable ailments.

This was a slum. The waste baskets had not been emptied in weeks. They stank of half-eaten sandwiches and takeaways. There was rubbish on the floor, papers strewn everywhere. Would you entrust your soul to a man who could not keep his world in order? Many did.

I found what I was looking for immediately. His report on me, left boldly on his desk for anyone and everyone to read. As he fully intended. I picked it up and have it with me now. Listen:

> I have tried deep analysis via techniques of Active Imagination, using the archetype of Lancelot of the Lake to access the imaginal nature of his psyche.
>
> I don't see this is as an autochthonous revival: that is, showing the tendency of primordial motifs to appear in all times and places. It seems more that this archetype has constellated in what Michael feels is a situation of need, gathering associational material from the world around and manifesting as this prime Hero archetype.
>
> The four functions of thinking, feeling, sensation, and intuition – all parts of the ectopsyche – have not all clicked into place. I feel that he is struggling toward his own process of individuation by trying to integrate unconscious contents into his own consciousness, thereby becoming a psychologically whole individual.
>
> He seems to spend his whole time wrestling with his urge toward numinosity, as experienced by his fascination for this activated archetype of Lancelot, and also with his own Shadow,

within which is collected all that he denies, fears and hates in himself.

He also has hallucinatory episodes in which mythic characters manifest in his day to day life. Originally I felt that there were elements of a crude Münchausen Syndrome in aspects of his behaviour but I have come to reject this hypothesis.

In summary, his is a classic example of 'Realization of the Shadow' whereby he seeks to grow fully, emotionally conscious of the Shadow's contents, although at this point he still cannot quite escape from a certain identification with the Shadow which – typically – produces a kind of amoral, inflated craziness.

That, bien sûr, was complete nonsense. I read the words out loud but they may as well have been in Urdu. They are noises, no more: Sir Bruce bashing his shield with his sword and hoping to impress or frighten people that way.

What enraged me was his summary that he had seen me twice a day for two hours, every day for almost two weeks. I have told you of our very brief, jousting encounters: was it three? four? No more than that. The man had hidden from me. Constantly.

And his conclusion:

Despite all my efforts I have been unable to get the slightest sense of who this patient that we call Michael actually is, or where he came from. He is a complete a mystery and I can go no further with him.

Of course he left this on the desk so that the Bad People would see it, believe that he had nothing to reveal, and leave him alone.

Fool. That he had even tried to engage with me, du Lac, was signing his own death warrant.

I was lying in the exact centre of the half-circle of the great lawn which lies before the Royal Crescent, at the other end of Brock Street from the Circus. Although fully clothed, I was bathing under the sun and trying to imagine that I was bathing in the waters of my own lake. Most unsatisying, but necessary. Fire is a difficult element for du Lac. Yet I need the warmth when tired. And I am so tired.

Then Kelvin appeared. Still clad in his ridiculously tight leathers. He circled my supine form, saying nothing. Saying everything. Scared.

Have you ever seen a whirlpool? A real one, not the kind you get in kitchen sinks. Morgana took me to see the monster at Corryvrecken once. We sat in the stern of her little blue boat. I cannot remember if we had a sail or used oars or her magic but we let the current take us. Her black hair blowing wildly as the waves beneath darkening storm clouds. I could see the vortex that we were spiralling into, and fancied that it carried up the noise of the boulders grinding on the sea-bed.

Are you afraid, big boy?

Would I admit such a thing to such a woman? My only fear has ever been that I might end my life without being re-united with Gwenevere.

Gulls flew above us – white comets against the sinister sky. Salt was on my lips and caking on my long eyelashes. With all my skill I remained imperturbable. To her eyes at least.

She screeched with laughter. Most unseemly. She was in her element, as they say now, without fully understanding such things. Water and Air. Truly, vraiment, she was insane.

When did this happen? Last year? Last century? It might have been during the times of the Old and Young Pretenders when I did some discreet work for both.

My squire finally stopped his own spiralling inward and looked down on me. His toes touching my heels so that I lay there like his own shadow. The sun at his back.

You know what's happened don't you? Sir?

I closed my eyes. Fées can often see things more clearly this way.

Tell me. Dites-moi.

It's McHaffee. Who you call Sir Bruce. He's dead.

I shook my head from side to side. Thrice. Sir Bruce will re-appear in some other guise. I will know him at once. I never knew this McHaffee.

He threw himself from the top of Bath Abbey.

I remembered the carving on the front, the ladder of climbing angels, and the one which is always falling off.

Perhaps he was thrown.

He gave a girlish squeak. Undignified. It would be a long time before this one would win his spurs.

Did you... did you do it?

What do you think?

I begin to think you're capable of anything. Did you?

Did I? The night before is still a blank to me. Deep sleep. No dreams. Yet if I wanted to kill the wretch who wore the legend of Sir Bruce I would have chosen a more fitting demise.

The boy knelt at my feet. The sun poured over my face. I sat up.

Squire Kelvin... some distance behind you, at one hundred metres exactement, there are two men in the trees and shrubs. Watching. Can you not feel their eyebeams through the binoculars? Do not turn and look!

He did not.

They are the men you thought were Mormons. They are, in fact, assassins.

Michael... Chevalier du Lac. Sir. I am very very scared. It's not a faery-tale with you any more.

Zut. With me, it is always a faery tale.

I do not know what day it is. It must be around Nones, although I can hear no bells. A short while ago I was sitting in the little café in the Guildhall indoor market. Near the centre of Bath. It is the sort of café that has the style of an earlier decade. With the same sort of menu. The Tommies that I have fought with many times would call it a place of Greasy Spoons although the spoons here are in fact spotless. It is not far removed in style from the estaminets that some of them would have visited for R&R between their stints in the trenches.

I sat in the corner in what is almost a painted pew. Around me were little stalls selling low quality bric-a-brac: what we French would term bibelots. Others selling used books. Confectionary. A barbershop. Crockery. Cheap jewellery. Pies. Electrical items. Clocks. Cheese. The canopies are boldly coloured or striped, alive with greens, reds, orange, faded gold. The place is almost medieval in tone and makes me quite nostalgic. I feel there should be jongleurs, jugglers or acrobats in harlequin outfits plying their trade amid the chaos of the narrow aisles.

I was keen – most keen – to see the Merlin. He has always turned up when I needed him, even if his advice has been edged toward being curious rather than useful. I even set a place for him here, opposite me. I have found, over the centuries, that the way to summon such beings from the vasty deeps is to proceed like this. There was a blue mug of tea with milk and four sugars steaming away for him.

When Merlin came I intended to offer him anything he wanted to eat. The cooks here looked at me quite strangely when I asked them if they had any fried nightingale or even lark's tongue, but they offered me ham, eggs and chips which were truly excellent. I ate mine – he would not mind me starting without him. His was set in place, opposite, along with the tea.

There was a hush about the market. They all recognised me when I came in. *Dulux*, they whispered. *It's Dulux*! They whispered it with delight, and some awe. Some of them burst into a gentle applause, thanking me for the work I had done to make their Kingdom of Gorre safe again. I am used to that. I was a celebrity 1500 years before the present siliconic oafs were born.

I drank my tea. Slowly. I needed soothing. I am not too proud to confess this to you – though I would never do so to a black priest! I peered into the depths of my steaming mug and knew that this was a miniature Lake. All parts of me could be glimpsed within, if I knew how to look. Listen, ecoutez, I did not learn to appreciate the delight and power of tea until my time in Flanders, during the never-ending battles for Ypres. It soothes me better than any of potions that the Merlin would dispense to the king. In truth, I have often wondered if those beverages and their mystic contents made the True Arthur degenerate into Arser. I will speak more of this soon.

I have the chess-piece of the Queen on the chequered table-cloth next to me. Last night, I used it to summon the spirit of Gwenevere to within touching distance.

I will explain. Listen…

Even Chrétien de Troyes and that teller of yarns Thomas Malory noticed that Gwenevere was always being kidnapped. They were partly right. I suppose I should not mock them, for they were writing many years after the events themselves. Not all the souls in the Faery realms wanted her associating with the Humans. They felt that such dalliance would make their own shining kingdom impure. They saw the Human world as dark and dirty, chaotic, constantly at war. Whatever benefits the Fées might gain from allying with them via Arthur were hardly worth it, in their golden eyes.

Some of them did indeed try to snatch their Queen back. I was called upon to stop them. I used no violence. They respected me, du Lac, who had grown up among them and beaten the faery crap out of large numbers timeless times without number.

But at other moments, perhaps when she was bored with Arser, I can only say that Gwenevere played games.

From somewhere, I have a memory of being made to watch a children's cartoon. On television. Something about wild races. There was a character – I recall her name with certainty – Penelope Pitstop, who kept getting trapped somewhere and calling out *Help! Help!* in a tiny voice. I am being disrespectful, perhaps, but that made me chuckle. It was so like Gwenevere. She was not trapped or endangered at all but she liked me riding up to rescue her and then – you can guess the rest.

But last night… Yes. Forgive me for rambling. Last night was difficult. I am not being vulgar but entirely ironic when I tell you that I, du Lac, had problems with water. It happens when the Fée side of me overbalances the Human. Often. The closer I get to Gwenevere the more does my Fée blood get agitated. And so my little apartement was beset with water disasters.

It started when I was holding the chess piece as the Merlin might hold his wand, trying to send my spirit out across the city. Hoping for a response. As a creature of Earth and Water it is not something I can do easily. Gwenevere herself, of Fire and Air, can do it easily, sending her spirit abroad like the beam of a torch. I struggle.

Yet the intensity of my effort broke all the seals in the equipment around me. Taps in the little kitchen started dripping, then pouring. The rainfall head of the shower did the same. A small trickle of water came toward me from under the washing machine that Kelvin was so necessarily expert with. Heavy rain from outside was seeping around the window frames and I noticed that the damp on the wall had formed a rough hexagonal pattern like the map of France.

I think the Water Elementals were trying to give du Lac power in his attempt to contact Gwenevere. Because of their connection with the Human side of me, some of them must have learned a degree of empathy. Perhaps. Some of the beings in the Fée World adore me as humans adore the Man Jesus – as some sort of Saviour. Others have always sought to crucify me – with lies.

But last night… last night… I held the chess piece tightly. I was angry with the world and its long drawn-out suffering. I called out:

You. Come. To. Me.

I was masterful. Perhaps I am no longer afraid of the woman I love?

As I was staring intently, punching out my thoughts, the walls before me suddenly dissolved and instead of the stone buildings of Brock Street I was looking, to my astonishment, into a warm place of birdsong, sun and trees. Into the Green World that is subtly deeper and greener than anything a mortal can know.

And there was Gwenevere, looking at me, worried.

Reproachful!

Why?!

What did she look like? Imagine a dazzle of light, a slim and perfect figure of half-transparent or opalescent air. From her heart ran a current of shining fire, pulsing through her body like electricity, and her hair waving and luminous, blowing all about her exquisite body like living strands of gold.

Come to me she said in her musical, silvery voice.

I always do. I always come to your rescue.

She laughed. My heart almost burst, it had been so long since I had heard that wondrous sound.

But I am not imprisoned. Not now.

I laughed. A deep, watery gurgle.

You tease me again. As always.

*My champion, my true love… it is **I** who have come to rescue **you**. You are –*

She never finished her words. There was a furious barking from outside, in the street. Many dogs. Belonging to the crusties who lurked around the abode of their hero Dulux. The glade returned to being a damp wall. The sun an electric light. Have I told you that I, du Lac, do not like dogs? Now I like them even less.

Despite the acute angle of vision from my apartement window onto the pavement below, I could see the blue lights of an ambulance and of one of those larger police vehicles that Kelvin termed a Paddy Wagon: for taking Bad People into custody. No doubt one of those that I had hospitalised recently will be demanding Human Rights compensation because he can no longer pick his nose with his little finger. I heard the front door open, people entering. It would have been wrong to do battle with those young people in uniform doing their duty. Sighing, still thrumming from my beautiful and brief encounter with Gwenevere, doing my best to suppress my slight tendency to self-pity, I left behind my leaking place and went downstairs to meet them.

In fact I never got that far. The door to the apartement below mine was flung open as I passed. A tall, slim, elderly and very elegant woman stood there in full evening dress as if she had just come from a grand ball.

Come here m'sieur. I implore you. Je vous demande!

When a woman implores du Lac in two languages then du Lac must do his best! I stepped into a room as small as mine, filled with books on every available place, but also crammed with exquisite Art Deco furniture and bibelots. I felt at home in this pseudo-French ambience.

She offered me wine. I declined. She gave a knowing purse of her thin lips and narrowed her eyes, but raised her own glass to me.

I know exactly who you are, m'sieur.

She said it teasingly.

Who? Qui?

You are the man that all women are looking for: who will protect and champion, and never scorn.

I said nothing. It was true.

Then who are you mam'selle? Qui êtes-vous?

She gave a little girlish giggle. Blushed.

I, my perfect gentle knight, am a child of Earth, but my race is of the starry heavens!

Her voice rose heavenward as she spoke. I remembered Kelvin telling me about her: 'Fruity as a nutcake' was his cruel comment. This was the woman who believed she had mated with Beings from other worlds. We were not so different, were we? I also had mated in realms that were not my own.

There was heavy, slow footfall on the stairs. Two, four, five people going up. Cautiously, reluctantly. It is instructive what an Old Soldier can tell from mere footsteps: three young vigorous men, one overweight older man, and a young but determined woman.

Ssssh!

We stood there, two statues, until the same number came down again. Quickly. Relieved to have found my place empty. Then the front door closed and the dogs yelped again before the two vehicles departed.

I am known in this life as Veronica Pursé-Coutts. I have met you many times before in previous lives.

We were never lovers!

I said this too forcibly perhaps but I was worried in case Gwenevere was able to eavesdrop from behind the thin veil that separates the worlds. I could not face her getting jealous again.

No, no, sir! Non non m'sieur! Your mind was always elsewhere, on another woman. I could see it in your eyes. Yet you rescued me un, deux, trois, quatre temps and went on your way when you could have ravished me. I always sensed that I was but a mere faint echo of your real and truest love.

That was true. It would have been ungallant of me to agree. I simply said:

Merci. And now I must leave you again, with thanks.

She gulped down the last of her wine and threw the glass over her shoulder against the wall, turning her back to me. I left quietly. Not only did I really need to speak to the Merlin, but also I had to get away before Veronica noticed the water pouring through her ceiling from my room above.

I ramble. Forgive me. It is an age thing. I wish I had known my father King Ban long enough to hear *him* ramble. Perhaps I am becoming like the person he would have been. So, at that moment there in the Guildhall market, the tea I had placed for the Merlin was lukewarm but still drinkable. Likewise the food: I put a plate over it to retain the heat. He had to come. Everyone in the café was looking at me.

Behind them, between them, fitting into the gaps between the normal shoppers and traders, the crusties, like shadows themselves, looked at me adoringly. I do not know what they want from me. At least they left their dogs outside.

What would they all think, I mused, when they saw the Merlin of Britain squeezing into the little pew? I put my hands on either side of my own blue mug, on the white plastic table cloth, observing the ripples. I closed my eyes. Bending my head toward the drink I whispered *Merlin* three times.

Then to my surprise I caught the smell of cheap aftershave. Approaching. Odd, I thought, as he usually smells of armpit. I opened my eyes. Slowly.

Unless the Merlin was shape-shifting (not for the first time!) or else had lost many kilos of fat, several kilometres of wrinkles and at least 15 centuries in age, this neatly dressed, clean-shaven young man in a smart suit with white shirt and grey tie and close-cropped hair was not him.

He spoke softly, carefully, looking anxiously to the people at every side.

Just acknowledge me. That's all I ask.

I furrowed my brow. How could I acknowledge anyone or anything when I did not know who or what it was that needed acknowledging? At least my native French with their innate logic would never get into this tangle.

The young man then sipped at the tea. Pulled a face. He clearly did not like the 4 sugars that the old magician always demanded. This was definitely not the Merlin shape-shifting. He went on, almost whining:

I've done all you wanted. I always did – when you were around. We can help each other.

He was mentally ill. Clearly. There seemed a lot of it about in Bath that summer.

*Look… I got rid of all the piercings, all the studs and dreadlocks. All my friends. At least give me some credit for trying to please you. And acknowledge **who** I am.*

It hit me then. Not as hard as a blunt lance into the chest, but more like a sharp bite from a small dagger: this was the Wild Man. I must have looked like a fish in one of my deepest lakes. I also looked to the crusties that he seemed to lead and noticed that many of them had shaved their heads to look like his. To look like mine.

I decided to fence with him. His skills would be primitive but every man has to learn some time.

But tell me first, m'sieur, who do you think I am?

There was long pause. He nodded toward the crusties, who were trying to be inconspicuous and so were completely conspicuous.

Some of them think you're an ex-pig. Ex-police, he added, though I had become familiar with the idiom thanks to my squire. *That you've seen the light and decided to fight the corrupt Establishment on their behalf. Some of them think you're a kind of avatar. They have stories of how you seem to disappear after having dealt with injustice. There are overlaps between the factions. A few of them think you're a trap. An agent provocateur. That if you bring them out into the light of day, by getting them to follow you, the pigs will be able to get them.*

Like Sir Bruce, I thought. Some of them see me as Sir Bruce! Had I taken his place already?

*But who or what do **you** see me as?*

I don't see, I know. I know that you're British Army. I know that you spent a lot of time overseas over the last 18 years. Or perhaps undercover. I know that you have had bad things done to you and probably done bad things in return. Which have damaged you, and your mind.

I frowned. This young man was clever. Not wholly right, but not entirely wrong. He had a bright, intelligent face. Handsome, almost. He reminded me strongly of someone though I could not say who. Gawaine? My cousins Lionel and Bors? He was like a leaping salmon as he took a deep breath and puffed out his chest:

But more than anything else I also know that you're my –

Well, I do not know what sort of demon he saw me as being because at that very moment there were great alarums and I found myself being approached by excited camera crews to the left and four earnest police officers to the right. Converging. No wonder the Merlin had kept away!

The crusties leapt from their shadows and formed a barrier.

No violence! cried the young man who was no longer Wild. Did he speak to them, or to the people seeking to reach me?

I finished the last drop of my tea, wiped my lips on the paper napkin, and made my escape through the side door. As an old soldier, such exits are always the first thing to prepare.

This young handsome stranger had the temerity to grab my shoulder before I disappeared. I was impressed.

She will see you tonight. 8 o'clock. Sham Castle.

Who?

Who do you think?

The alarums increased. I went.

I am sitting here at the gate of what they call Sham Castle. I am not sure when the time of 8 p.m. occurs, exactly, so I came here after Sext and have been brooding ever since, at the centre of the pointed arch.

What am I brooding about? It is because all the books written about me have ensured that I am remembered for four things:

Being the greatest knight in the world.

Being Gwenevere's lover and thus my king's betrayer.

Being denied the Holy Grail.

Going insane for love.

But there is also a fifth, according to some: Being used by Mordred to cause a civil war and bring Camelot crashing.

That last has a worm of truth in it but no more. Let it wriggle away from us.

It is a strange and aptly named place this sham of a castle: no more than a single white wall with a central pointed arch flanked by two high circular turrets, and two square towers at each end. The gate in which I sit leads to and from nothingness. It was designed and built as a folly only yesterday – in Faery terms. In Human terms, it is over 200 years old. Some rich man's attempt to evoke the world in which I once lived, of which he must often have dreamed.

Yes it is a fake – a partial truth, but it is strangely familiar. I cannot say why. Then again, I have waited at the gates of many castles. Over many centuries. I have also been locked in many dungeons – particularly when I went insane.

How did that happen? Was it the endless warfare? Some cunning torture arranged by Sir Bruce? No, it was caused by Gwenevere.

Whatever the source of the True Arthur's glamour, he began to lose it. That was my fault. Perhaps. I think he had as much need of the White Shadow as myself. She gave him his power, even if he thought it was all within himself, and his alone.

She would never tell me what the sex was like between them. Her loyalty toward him hurt, but I would not have changed that. She had taken her oaths and few souls are as damned as oath-breakers. Yet because of her love for me, and our secret trysts, I du Lac damned her. For myself, I swore to protect the True Arthur's kingdom. There was no mention of staying away from his wife, though I tried. I tried hard. Exceedingly hard.

After a while, perhaps to get some balance or justice in his life, he took a mistress and had a son. Then his half-sister Morgana used her magical whiles to get into his bed and get pregnant, resulting in the bastard Mordred. Who grew up to be a fine man, incidentally, and a worthy successor to the man who was now just a pale shadow. Do not believe all you read about Mordred.

The whole of the kingdom knew all these supposed secrets of the court but said nothing out loud. The place seemed to be filled with scribes.

We, the True Arthur and du Lac, who were so much alike that we could have been brothers, started to drift apart. In the early days we had shared much in the way of fun, laughter, danger and slaughter when establishing his kingdom. Then, unspoken and undiscussed, we developed skills that kept us subtly distant even when fighting back to back. It was like chain mail: you could see through the links to the flesh behind, but you could not penetrate, or feel much warmth. We became formal. Our relationship continued from the neck upward. Our grins became fixed. Our greetings stilted.

Did he know of my envies which drowned my agonies of guilt?

Did he sense my hatred when he took Gwenevere off to his bed with a bear-like *Grrrrrrr...*?

Did he gloat at the pain I felt when I saw her go with him, apparently gaily?

Those were the days when I sat in my empty room and learned to create and don armours which were not of iron or steel, but far tougher than either.

Then he made great fuss of his new favourites. Younger knights. Though none of them as handsome as me. One of them was deemed to be my own son by Elaine, who had been given my true name: Galahad.

Gwenevere, who was unable to have children, hated the boy. I sometimes think that she and Merlin conspired to create the whole sham of the Holy Grail to get rid of the bastard.

Zut alors but I fought great battles for my king. I took an army into Gaul and beyond to drive away the Saracens who would have ravaged Britain and tortured my Queen. By fighting these battles I kept away from the love. I fought more and more. I fought and killed because of the love that I could not control. The only thing I had to remind me of Who I am and always must be was my ring, bearing the legend Love Begets Love. Does this speak to the Human in me or the Fée? I have sometimes thought they are the cruellest words.

And then I returned to Britain. Just before Pentecost. No great crowds greeted me at the gates of Camelot as they had always done in the past, though Merlin gave me a sad, knowing look as I rode past.

The pennons in the Great Hall were wearing thin, their colours faded. The straw underfoot was dirty and uneven and matted with dog-shit. The king himself was chubby, all too human. His hair was grey, eyes watery. Where he had once seemed bold, now he was brash. Had I outgrown his wisdom or had it always been no more than crassness? The True Arthur had long gone, a generation ago. Now Arser had taken his place.

I looked at Gwenevere standing next to him. Hand in hand. I knew at once that she would never leave him, and I would never understand. Her heart was of pure diamond. I think it still is. But my heart of wax melted at that moment and so did my mind.

Here at Sham Castle I knew that a woman was approaching me from behind. I could also smell her perfume as acutely as I could once smell the gun-oil of the Schmeisser sub-machine guns of the Waffen SS. This was considerably more appealing however. White Musk. Liberally splashed. Any normal man would have been instantly aroused but I, du Lac, was dismayed. This could not be Gwenevere, who had no body odour and thus no need for perfumes. This could only be:

Hello Elaine. It has been a long time. Centuries?
She said nothing. Walked slowly around to face me.
Seems like it.

Then with a deep sigh she sat down next to me and we stared out over the serried rooftops of Bath, which were so much like wavelets on a lake. I looked at her out the corner of my left eye: she had hair of spun light, pouring onto the shoulders of her red summer dress. She had golden sandals which she removed, caressing her feet in the thick grass. It had often been noted at Camelot that she strongly resembled Gwenevere, though I could never see that.

It was a long silence but not entirely awkward. We had done this many times before. As Malory tells it, we had once had a home together that we called Joyous Gard, though our marriage was as much a sham as this castle. My heart and mind were always elsewhere. My body often followed them. When we were together we would sit in silence and hid behind armours of politeness and deference. Kindness too, I would add.

You can't go on like this.

I nodded but thought it best to say nothing. The Fée side of me was fading. The Human was becoming old.

Gil is determined to get through to you. He sees you as a casualty of war.

Gil?

Your son, Gilead. At least you managed to make him smarten himself up. I never could. He hero-worships you. Not that you spent any time with him. As he grew up you were more dream than reality. Always off somewhere, fighting the bad guys as you said. Bad guys or Saracens.

Gilead? This must be her diminutive for Galahad. I knew I had to be very careful here. There were cold wavelets of concern splashing onto me, into me. I know not why.

A handsome young man, Elaine.

Like his dad.

*How is **your** father?*

She looked at me oddly, shrugged.

He died last year. Can you even remember him?

A keen fisher. He hated me.

(He was indeed the Fisher King. A friend of the fat Merlin. Thought he knew everything but knew nothing. No-one dared tell him. I did not dare tell Elaine.)

I wouldn't say 'hated'. You used to take him to the disabled fishermen's place at Tucking Mill. He was grateful for your efforts.

We looked across toward the setting sun. Huge white clouds rolled and tumbled and turned red under its rays.

You asked to meet me here for our first date. I asked you: Why here? You told me you wanted to be my knight in shining armour. I was 17, I'd never known anyone as romantic as you. Strong, mysterious. And that uniform...

I did not remember that. When you are semi-eternal and in love with the eternal Gwenevere, such babble can float away from memory. I said nothing.

Remember that you told me your name was Knight, with a 'kay', not Night as in darkness. That your first name was Handsome.

I did not remember that conversation either. Again, I said nothing. She stared into the distance, into watery depths of her own memory. There was a touching wistfulness about her tone.

Then you told me that your first name, Alain, was French for Handsome. You were such a tease. Though a nice one. You said that your favourite word was 'gallant'. That you loved reading about history and that you were adopted, so you never knew your real parents.

That is indeed the case. But did I allow her to call me that? Eh bien I would rather be called Alain than Lancelot.

You told me that you'd be my Knight in Shining Armour, forever. How could a young girl resist?

Indeed.

And then you had me against that wall...

Elaine!

A classic British Army Knee Trembler as you told me afterward.

Get a grip Elaine!

That's what you said then, too.

She was not looking at me, she was looking into some distorted mirror of her own past. Teasing me. Perhaps.

But it didn't last more than one minute, and when I got pregnant it all changed. Didn't it?

You know I had oaths.

You and your oaths! There were four of us in our marriage: me, you and fucking Queen and Country.

Well, she got that right, although I deplored her language. To my surprise, I felt myself being somewhat afraid of this woman. Did that mean I had some sort of love for her? In truth, I think her own fée blood was faltering: we get our time-sense confused, diluted and stretched. And place-sense too. Although this Sham Castle was undeniably familiar to me I knew it was merely an echo of the real thing, long ago. Elaine was undoubtedly a fine-looking specimen but I worried that she was somewhat gaga, bless her.

Look you mad bastard, I know you've had bad things done to you. Gil reckons you've been used and brainwashed by a corrupt Establishment. I don't care, just come home with me. Let me help you. Forget your Queen and Country. Come out of the shadows.

What could I say? This woman, to whom I had been married for centuries, was exquisite if slightly insane. Yet she was giving me love that was entirely undeserved. It would be neither manly nor gallant were I to demolish her words.

In the event I was rescued by the sight of Kelvin on his palfrey, riding along the road below. He saw us and waved. Shouted.

Sir! Sir!

Elaine shook her head and sighed. *You've got him playing your games now, have you?*

Elaine I must go.

How often have I heard that before?

I stood up and walked down the slope toward my squire. Elaine called after me:

I won't wait forever. And you'll have to prove yourself. To me. And if you ever go anywhere near that old cow again I'll rip your balls off. Now take this:

Although I was rattled by her description of Gwenevere as an old cow I had to show some understanding of what she had suffered in terms of jealousy and betrayal. I did that by staying mute. Then she handed me a slip of paper with what looked like one of Merlin's incantations on it: **www.fatbastardgitmerlin.org.uk**. *Those are not the real words of power, you understand. I would not have you getting blasted through meddling. But they are close enough.*

You said I had to give this to you when all else seemed lost.

Nothing is lost, I said firmly, though I was confused by all her words.

And you might wanna to change that suit of yours. It's getting very grubby. You've got a wardrobe full of very good stuff at home.

I was startled to see a flash of gold in her eyes.

My squire seemed jolly after his recent terrors. He sat astride his palfrey in a lively manner. Clearly, he had something of delight to tell me. The sun caught the edges of his white leather outfit and limned him with fire. He looked absurd. Especially when he took off his helmet and held it on his lap like a begging bowl.

Oh. You. Tease. he said.

I frowned. I was still thinking of Elaine's strange comments.

McHaffee wasn't thrown from the top of Bath Abbey.

I never said so.

He just had a heart attack.

Just? Sir Bruce had no heart.

But it was just a normal heart attack. You didn't kill him.

I never said that I did.

Then those assassins – they were just you having a laugh. God, you had me going didn't you?

There are no assassins.

You admit it?

Squire Kelvin, I will tell you a story as the fat Merlin might tell it. Come to your own conclusions.

His face lit up. He sat on his palfrey like a young girl, side-saddle. Unzipped his outfit from throat to navel, slowly, and winked. Why, I do not know. Most unseemly.

I'm sitting comfortably. Sir. So begin.

There was man, strong and handsome. Let us call him Alain. He was approached one night in his small, damp but chic apartement by two Very Bad People. With his supernatural senses he knew they were creeping up the staircase. Quietly. Confidently. Thinking they only had an ageing soldier to deal with.

Instead of the best knight in the world. Oh I like this story!

Quiet. They thought this 'Alain' was asleep, slouched in his armchair, slumped forward. As the first Bad person approached with the garrotte, Alain, with the vision of fées, knew exactly where he was. Judging the distance perfectly he merely sat up straight and swung the heavy copper-bottomed saucepan that he had between his legs in a pure and perfect killing arc. The first Bad Person died instantly.

And the second? Did he get dispatched the same way?

The second Bad Person was less Bad than the first. He was merely a novice like yourself, learning his trade. He was astonished, paralysed.

Suddenly incontinent of urine. He should never have worn those summery trousers. He had never seen brains before, or had them splashed upon his face.

Then?

Alain felt sorry for him. With his incomparable speed he threw the wretch to the floor and broke only his arm then removed the idiot's radio and spoke to the Badder People who gave him his pitiful orders.

Saying what?

That it ends now. That if anything should ever happen to Alain or any of his family or friends or squire, then every court in the land, every newspaper, would have instant knowledge of Bad Things that they had done. But if they left him and his family alone, forever, they would be safe. They had his word, his most sacred oath.

So what happened to the body? Why was there no mention of it in the news?

There are Dark Powers in the Human World who would instantly clean up such mess. As if it never happened. People can simply disappear. Without explanation.

I was thinking of Galahad and Perceval of course.

So did you – I mean 'Alain' – murder Princess Diana? Does he still have this hanging around him?

Why ask me!? Perhaps it was those two assassins who did it. Only the fat Merlin will ever know the full story, and only the High Born will ever be told.

That was brilliant story.

He saluted me. Ridiculous. I broke off the aerial from his palfrey. *Kneel*, I told him.

Ooh…! but he knelt. I touched him with the rod on each shoulder.

You have won your spurs. Your work for me is finished. Arise Sir Kelvin.

He rose.

God I love you.

Sir Kelvin I am not God – though it is an understandable mistake. What does this silly name Kelvin mean incidentally?

It means 'handsome' actually.

Really?

Vraiment!

You are taking le piss. Yet, it is fitting. Now go… your own Quests await.

I made to kiss him in the French way: one on each cheek, but he sought to intercept my mouth with his tongue. I gave him a last slap, but a gentle one. He loved it.

Using skills that are innate to me, and which I once taught to the newly-formed commandos at Spaen Bridge in the 1940s, I disappeared into the trees and shrubbery lining the road. I could see Elaine approaching and Kelvin clearly waiting to accost her. I wanted to know what either might say. I hid. I listened.

Excuse me madam. Can I have a quick word?

No, she said and carried on past. He dismounted and scurried along next to her. I followed them silently, moving like a panther through the greenery.

That man you were talking to... you know him don't you?

I wasn't talking to any man.

Ah but Elaine was clever! She also spoke the truth. It was a fée she spoke to, not a hu-man.

Oh come on, I don't mean him any harm. I just want to know who he really is.

*So who are **you**?*

I'm Kelvin. I was his keyworker at that half-way house. His carer.

Elaine bent at the waist and shrieked with laughter. Carried on laughing. I had forgotten she did that.

His carer? You? His carer? Do you have any idea – no no, of course not. His carer... HIS carer! Oh my oh my...

She was capitalising me as she spoke, like some people did with The Man Jesus.

Oh ha ha hardi ha. I saw you together. You know him.

Do I?

You were talking to him.

Was I?

Come on, tell me who he is. Who he really is.

Dunno what you mean.

He tells everyone he's Lancelot of the Lake, or du Lac as he prefers it.

Does he? That's nice.

Or did he really assass-

Elaine used incredible speed to clamp her hand over his mouth.

Mam'selle, careless talk costs lives, she told him. I was impressed. Not only had she told the truth but, with her atrocious French accent, she took the piss out of him and his girliness at the same time. I have under-rated her. Perhaps my fée vision was not so complete after all.

Don't do that… Please tell me. I give you my oath that I won't blab. The man's a complete a wind-up merchant or a bit of nutter or both but I love him. I really do.

That's nice. Doesn't everyone love the great du Lac?

I liked that. She was saying everything and saying nothing. A true soldier's wife. Perhaps I had under-rated her over the centuries.

He says he's semi-eternal.

That's nice too.

Please, please… who is he really?

Listen sonny, and listen carefully. Perhaps he's exactly WHO he says he is. Now bugger off.

She made an obscene gesture to me over her shoulder without looking, as she walked off. She had known I was there all along. I was impressed.

Bath Central Library. A place of high ceilings and high minds. Had I not been a warrior I might have been a scholar. If I had turned my fighting skills into scholarship I would have been the cleverest – and handsomest – savant the Human world has ever known. I would have attracted as many enemies and fought as many battles and probably have gone to the stake for my learning. That is another way of being a warrior, and one I deem far nobler than my own calling.

There was a row of computer terminals. A couple of people were busy at them but they left the moment they saw me. I do not know why. On the other hand one of the librarians approached me, quite boldly, with a distinct but very Human sparkle in her eye. She wore a uniform and had clearly taken an oath to serve Bath City Council. We were allies immediately.

Oh my word if it isn't the great Dulux she exclaimed, in a pure Welsh accent. I had had many adventures in the Pen y Fan area, so I knew the dialect well. I gave a slight courtesy bow and also looked at her name badge:

Then it is the great Siân Perkins I countered, and she sort of squirmed as she giggled. Her eyes were melting. She clearly adored me. I am used to such. It is not easy being the handsomest knight of all time. *Are you from Tir na nÓg, that paradise beyond the setting sun?*

Port Talbot, actually.

An easy mistake to make, mam'selle.

Gerraway you charmer! It's hard to believe you beat the crap out of my nephew. In the waiting room at the train station.

I do not apologise. He was being ungallant toward a vulnerable lady. A nun. Who had taken an oath to serve.

He deserved it. Do him again! He's blabbing to everyone that next time he'll come back with the whole rugby team.

Tell him to bring the reserves too, aussi.

Aussi… she giggled. I do not know why.

Show me how to use this, Siân Perkins, and bring me that scanning device on your own machine.

She did so, being swayed by my good looks as so many have been over the years. I watched the process of 'booting up', as the English say. It seemed strangely familiar.

Are there any more at home like you? she whispered to me, out of the corner of her mouth.

Siân Perkins. You wear a wedding ring and so have taken an Oath. Behave yourself.

The first screen appeared. A cartoon of a black knight and white knight charging each other on powerful destriers and the white knight – bien sûr – unhorsing the other. Again and again. Seven times. A small empty box appeared at the bottom of the screen.

It looks like you need a bar code said my adoring lady-in-waiting, as if this magical encounter was the most natural, everyday thing in the world. Perhaps it was in Port Talbot.

I had to tear my sleeve. My excellent shirt had been washed by Kelvin on too high a setting. It had shrunk very slightly so it curved tightly against my great muscles.

Stop whimpering ma cherie I suggested. *And please do not lean against me.*

I scanned my inner bicep and then an image beeped on the computer screen as if I was looking outward from the inside of a knight's helmet, the eye-slot demanding a password. Five letters.

Using my incredible speed, so that my companion could not see, I typed in: d.u.l.a.c. When I pressed Enter it made a noise like an axe striking a shield. It was not correct.

Siân Perkins... leave me alone for a moment. I need to think.

She did so, and then I dived into deep waters of thought by staring down at my heart.

If it was not a case of WHO I was but WHO I served, what should I input?

Eh bien, I have only ever served the highest and that came before Protector or Guardian or Champion of the King. As ordained by my foster mother Nimué, I am the priest of the goddess Diana, in whose sacred groves along the shores of Lake Nemi I became the mighty du Lac. So the five letters just had to be: d.i.a.n.a. When I pressed Enter, I did indeed then enter a realm I had never expected.

What did I see?

I saw:

An old home movie. A young boy – 3? 4? – running across a grassy meadow next to a stream. He ran straight toward the camera calling *Daddy Daddy*. A handsome little boy. The person holding the camera has a familiar but strangely unnerving laugh. The camera shakes, he is laughing so much.

Then I saw:

A young woman sitting on the same grass, her back to the camera, dipping her bare legs into the stream. There is a picnic basket next to her. A black and white chequered cloth on which lay white paper plates, triangular sandwiches of white bread. A bottle of wine – unopened – and two bottles of blue fizzy drinks. A big red beach ball.

Disneyland soon, Gil, Paris Disney. Dad's got time off. Oui Oui! Allons!

I see the young woman turn. It is Elaine, of course. A fine looking woman then too. She looks toward the camera. She raises her eyebrows and laughs.

You're a nutter Alain...

I saw:

Many things. Warm things. Inexplicable things. I might have

pulled out the plug of the computer but felt that I must watch, and try and fathom these mysteries of the Human world.

I remembered that thing the fat Merlin did with the two mirrors, when I saw strings of du Lac, each one with a separate path and sometimes overlapping destiny. Was that this century? This millennium? Or perhaps only a matter of weeks ago? Is this Merlin's way of showing me how it could have been for one of them?

I saw no relevance to my own situation. I wondered again if all the du Lacs were not strung out through time but happening at once. Yet I envied that singular monsieur Knight with all of my two hearts.

I emerged from the library, oddly shaken. I intended to make my way back toward the great rushing weir that is the Sword Bridge and cross it to escape from Gorre. Sometimes, there is no shame in tactical retreat and I would surely find Gwenevere from another direction. Perhaps.

A large black car pulled up next to me, stopping all the cars coming down Walcot Street. Even though the traffic light was green the driver did not move. He ignored the raucous horns of the vehicles behind so I knew that there was some Mission involved. The window in the rear wound down.

Hello big boy! called Morgana. *Get in you big lunk. I'll take you to see someone.*

I slid in next to her. She was beaming. It was like moonlight on sea – coming right into my face. She was calm and deep now, but often she can be stormy. She also held up a little vial of liquid.

You know that I can't let you see where I take you. I'd ask these goons in the front to hoodwink you but they're a bit scared. You're a legend, you know. And lunatics are said to have the strength of ten men.

Du Lac has the strength of 20.

Oh sweetie, I really have missed your crap. Drink this. Non-alcoholic. Filled with yummy vitamins and lots of useful E numbers.

It was murky. I shook the vial. Sniffed. The liquid was odourless.

Where is the fat git Merlin?

'M' darling doesn't want to see you. You always wind him up. He hates you calling him Merlin.

That was a matter of security of course. Yet I would never blab his name in front of anyone likely to cause trouble.

He's also very sensitive about his weight. But, believe me cherub, he's cleared up an awful lot of your shit behind the scenes.

I, du Lac, have never shit behind the scenes. Always in appropriate soldierly places. Perhaps I muddied the waters in a few places but nothing I could not live with. I shook the vial again and sniffed it again.

Is this what you gave McHaffee?

McHaffee? Just drink it, sweetie. Trust me.

Where are you taking me?

To see the one you love to hate and hate to love.

Will 'she' be there?

Oh you and your True Love. I must try it someday. Just drink, loverboy.

I drank. I was suddenly too weary to be wary. I think my Human side was taking over. I felt tired. Drained. Lakes can drain you know, if the underlying rocks gets fractured. Yawning, I put my head in her lap.

You handled it all brilliantly she whispered, stroking my head. *Pretending to be mad to take the heat off you. Making sure everyone knew you. Hiding in plain sight. Brilliant. A real diamond geezer, yet soft as putty inside. I know you. Not many do.*

Bien sûr, I fell asleep to the smell and sound of the blood in her lap which has the smell and sound of the sea.

I found myself with a fuzzy head, waking in a white, almost cubical room. Windowless. Air conditioned. A row of piercing lights inset into the ceiling. The purest place I had ever seen. No germs could possibly breach this citadel, much less Bad People. Utterly sterile. Utterly dead.

Except for Arser. Asleep. The man I loved to hate and hated to love, as Morgana said, not without insight.

Here he was on a stainless steel hospital bed with small lances threaded into his veins and masses of electronic equipment giving out information that I did not understand – other than to understand that he was not dead. Just sleeping. He was aware of nothing, no-one.

I do not know where this was. There are many places in Britain and Gaul that claim to have the True Arthur sleeping under a hill, waiting for the Summons. Then he would awaken, rise, and gallop out to rescue the world again.

Merde! This was not the man who drew me to Logres in the first place, my equal in every way. This was not a king but a failure. Look. Regardez!

Now where was Gwenevere? No wonder she was trapped. No-one, Human or Fée, not even du Lac could escape a prison like this.

Then I heard her voice behind me:

Don't turn around.

I turned around. I felt as if someone stronger than myself had punched me. I reeled. Perhaps it was the drug Morgana had given me.

Gwen... Jenny...

I was shocked. Utterly. When fées do begin to age they do so more rapidly than Humans, having none of the unguents or stratagems to keep skin smooth and hair silky. Yet this woman – who was she? She looked a pale shadow of the near-immortal White Shadow I had loved for so long. Skinny. Gaunt, even. Lank hair that was grey rather than silver-shot-with-gold. She wore a drab dress with long sleeves that might cover up needle marks, for all I knew. Had they treated her so badly in her prison? Time was coming to an end. I had to tell her, the simplest but deepest of truths:

I loved you.

She closed her eyes and shook her head as if to free it from my words.

But I also loved him! You led him astray. Turned him into a drunkard.

He became a drunkard to blot out what we were doing.

He became a drunkard because he loved you more than me. Did you never guess? The whole of our circle knew.

In truth there were never any secrets in Camelot. But no, I never guessed.

I could not take in what I saw. She was a wreck. The pressures of monarchy must have been too great. It was her timeless, ageless spirit which had been coming to me. I saw no echoes in this 'all too human' body. She saw my expression. Read it like a book, like the Little Book of Great Enchantment with the blank pages that everyone fills in with their own visions.

I'm sorry she said. Sorry for what, I do not know.

Was that all it was between us? Supernatural beauty and holy sex? I remembered that the only criticism she ever made of the True Arthur was done behind his back once, indicating with her little finger that he had a small prick. I felt smug then, knowing that my great lance satisfied her fully. Now, at the end of my endless Quest, I felt sick. The author of that anonymous book 'Lancelot of the Lake' was surely right when he insisted that I had loved her a thousand times more than she ever loved me.

They've been good to him here, kept him alive. If that's what you call this.

But you have to end it now. Do it, please. As I'm his wife they won't switch him off without my permission. I want you to do it. I can't.

Jenny...

Do it! If you've ever had any love for me, and want to help, then switch all that off. And then it ends. And we'll both be free.

She turned. The door was not locked. Had it ever been? She went and I did not try to stop her. The door closed like the final page of a little boy's faery story.

What did I feel and think as I looked at Arser? He who had once been kingly, and as strong as myself, was little better than a skeleton. Sunken cheeks. A green tinge. The smell of shit around him.

I had failed my goddess Diana. Misused my light. Acted out of anger at the wrong time. He, this Arser, had failed his whole kingdom. We had done bad things to Bad People and hoped that would make us good. There were things we *had* to do, Saracens to fight, but his anger for me made him lose all balance. He did not share my faith. He made noises about leaving the Quest and finding The Man Jesus, and he was in thrall to the Merlin anyway. We became like two knights trying to maintain their balance on cracking ice over a deep tarn. He asked once:

What if your precious Diana was about to betray you – all of us?

Whenever he spoke of betrayal and trust and oaths he was always alluding to the Holy Trinity that was himself, myself and Gwenevere. He thought he was God, and acted like it in our last days. Plus I think he was trying to do to me what I had done to

Ahasuerus: make me doubt my Goddess, my very reason. I never knew what to say. I put on armour and said nothing. Rien. Jamais. When he got damaged at our last battle, or Camlann as Malory called it, and about which I can never speak, I could only turn and cross my own Wasteland in search of that White Shadow I had lost.

And I have been wandering, questing, ever since.

I took out the chess piece of the Queen that I had carried for so long. Rested it on his puny chest, above his heart, finding a space amid the forest of wires. It rose and fell, weakly. He was kept alive by machine power now. He was no longer a Human. Bastard, I said, though I could have said anything and he would not have heard.

The door opened. Morgana came into the room. Put her hand on my shoulder.

Do it big boy she said, not unkindly. *You know you must. It all ends now. He was a rotten shag anyway.*

I leaned forward and balanced the tip of my finger on the tip of the switch. I flipped it. I did not look back as he gasped his last. An unhuman, machine-generated gasp. Morgana took my hand as if I was a little boy. I was grateful for that. Somehow. I am a King's son, and the King is dead. So I too am a King. I am Arser's equal at last. The knowledge does not help. I told her:

Let's go. Allons…

I am awake. On a bench beside the Abbey yard. It is night. The neon is glistening on the damp stone. My clothes are not fully wet so I cannot have been here long. I do not know how long ago Morgana gave me her witch-potion. Hours? Days? Years? I look at the clock on the Abbey. It says 11.35 and I understand what it tells me.

My Human side is now dominant. I feel as if I have lost something precious. My eternal youth, perhaps.

The wind blows a couple of red and white party balloons toward me, tied by a green string, bouncing them lightly at my feet. I try to grab them but I have lost my incredible speed. Despondent, I reach inside my shirt and peel off the duct tape. It removes chest hairs and I wince. The forget-me-nots I tried to preserve have shrivelled into stalks.

Human, all too Human I say out loud.

I look at the ring given to my Nimué, millennia ago: *Love begets Love.* Well I have fought many battles in Love's name. Have I sometimes confused Love with Oaths and Duty? Are they interlinked? I do not know. I am not as certain about the worlds as I once was. I think that a part of me can also be known, now, as Alain Knight, and live in a small cottage with a large pond, in a wood near here. Somewhere.

I hear a commotion from the narrow street which leads to where I sit. Once, I could have told you how many were coming, their purpose, and how confident in their approach. Now I can only guess from the rugby songs that they are slightly drunk and that they have won their match by a handsome margin. They swagger around the corner, the front rank arm-in-arm.

Wah hey! cries the central man. *It's that fuckin' lunatic Dulux. You done my little brother last week.*

He was 6 foot 4.

Well I'm 6 foot fuckin' seven. Try me you old git.

I count them. 8. When I had my power it would have been an even fight. To be fair, half of them try to mediate, try to drag him away. The rest are up for giving me a 'good kicking' as they slur it.

Come on then, he snarls. *You lot watch and learn. I won't kill 'im.*

He is young and angry and very large, but I know he is not a Bad Person, just an Arsehole.

Something clutches at my heart. Something new. Is this the fear that Humans feel at times like this? The only fear I ever knew was that which the Merlin described – the fear of the woman I loved. Yet this sort clutches my wax heart and crushes it out of shape just as easily.

Stand up you bastard.

The others, lower in the pecking order, mutter *leave it Gareth, leave it* – though I am not sure what 'it' is. But two others step forward. I know the play is to grab me. There is still distance between us. 20 metres perhaps. Still time to turn and run. I start to rise but…

A stubby hand clutches my shoulder from behind and pushes me back down.

No don't, no you don't says a voice. A woman's voice with the faint hint of a speech impediment. I glance around in surprise.

Grace!

The thugs pause. They act amused. There is enough humanity to want to see how this will play out. So do I!

Go 'way she snarls at the mob. It is a good snarl.

Go fuck yourself mongo comes a retort. *Nobody else will.*

I bristle. I gnash my still perfect teeth and find myself breathing heavily.

Grace, you must run. I cannot let you get hurt.

*I not let **you** get hurt.*

What was it Nimué called tears? The 'water of the heart'? I feel them springing now. Is my heart wax or diamond? I do not know. But it is beating very hard.

Come on then Dulux and Mongo. I'll do you both. Think two of you will do anything?

Well three actually, comes another voice. *Yah, that might be enough.*

Kelvin comes and stands next to us, a knight in white leather and the helm to match!

Kelvin! You do not have to do this.

I do. I took a personal oath that I would always be there if you needed me. Besides, your suit definitely needs to be dry-cleaned soon.

This was getting silly. Absurd. Typically English. I hear myself speak, eliding my words for the first time in centuries:

You're a nutter you are. You're a maniac.

Mais oui, says Sir Kelvin. *Certainement. Ha ha hardi hah…*

Is he becoming the knight I once was? Had he always been? Before us, Gareth was getting annoyed:

Okay – one old git, one fat moron and a raving poofter. Come on, I'll give the three of you first punch, how's that?

*What about the **four** of us?*

I turn again. There is a young man in uniform, carefully putting his boxes of warm pizzas on the bench next to me.

I owe you he whispered. *You saved my arse last week. I'm crap at fighting but I'll do my best.*

And you're not leaving me out either comes yet another voice from the night. And there is… well, Gilead.

Hello… son I say, finally. He glows. Am I shrinking or does he increase in size?

You're my dad, admit it.

I take a deep breath but it comes easily to me now:

I'm that. I am.

My fine looking son's eyes glisten with gold, his fée blood showing through.

The mob leader is bewildered: *For fuck's sake, how many more nonces, perverts, lunatics and cripples are there?*

Well what about that lot? asked Gilead with pleasant confidence, pointing to the shadows behind them. Out of which emerge a mass of the unalive ones who now seem very much alive. They all love me. There is a glint of gold their eyes too. I must get to know them some time.

Gareth and his cronies look around. Their mood has changed, they form into a tight knot rather like the old testudo or 'tortoise' the Legions would form for self-defence.

Yet it is still not finished because young Constable Godfrey comes strolling past.

Evenin' all he says in a mock tone, doing that bend of his knees that panto policemen do. *Nice night for it!*

Hey hey hey copper, arrest him! says Gareth his finger pointing at me like a lance. *That's Dulux. The one you're all after. There he is! Arrest him!*

Arrest who? Don't see a soul. Run along to your mammies, little boys, and walk quietly as you do.

He strolls off whistling, swinging an imaginary truncheon.

I rise and turn to face my circle of Good People.

Grace... Your name should be Majesty. I have never seen a braver soul than you. And the rest of you. But I cannot fight any more, I cannot do it, I'm...

Bollocks, says Kelvin with his unseemly use of language. *I'll tell you WHO you are. We all know. We've always known and always will. You are the great du Lac. The handsomest, best knight in the Holy Realm of Logres. The finest fighting man of all time. Just stand still for a moment, mon chevalier blanc. Bit of psycho-drama coming up!*

He does things with his hands, miming the putting on of armour, and somehow I feel the familiar weight, protection, and substance – though I keep him away from doing a cod-piece at which he does his inane *Ha ha hardi ha...* Somehow – I cannot say how – it becomes real and there I am with my white armour and the red band which *they* could all see if no-one else could.

Then Grace put her hand to my chest, my heart, where I always did my thinking. I am not sure if she poured something into me or I transmitted it to her. Perhaps this energy of 'du Lac' is in all of us, always, but needs to be coaxed from the depths.

They are all looking at me. There is light in their eyes.

One last teensy-weeny battle – Dad. Then you can come home.

Deep breath, deep breath. I rise from depths. A cold wind springs up.

Merci. Thank you.

I know now that I must stop agonising about semi-eternal souls and ancient deeds. I must savour this exquisite droplet of the present moment. This is better than winning through to the plastic Holy Grail. These dark shadows of the earth and of its humans are just as pure as the White Shadow that is Gwenevere and her kind.

Could I face one last battle? Certainement!

No killing I cry – though on the crest of a little laugh.

Oh Christ, oh fuckin' hell… mutters Gareth who sees me now, as WHO I am, stripped of my Oaths but shining and bold despite this.

I will stop him swearing. I will extract a simple oath from him – and the rest – that they will never insult a woman again no matter how old, how frail, or how uncomely they might seem. I will remove their blinkers and get them to see the gentle fée spirit in everyone.

But first I will give them all such a slapping that it will be passed down through their DNA to generations yet unborn who will marvel that their ancestors were once taught how to be truly human by a fée.

I turn to the fool Gareth and his very nervous gang and feel the light of stars surging through my veins. Laughing, I stride forward once more with my powerful faery gait as if I am under water, and we all cry out as one because we *are* all One. We cry the name that inspired the Good People how to fight and be just, how to be protective to the weak and how to be passionate in love: the name which made the Bad Ones and little shits wake sweating and shaking from their night terrors, screaming:

Du Lac!

Lightning Source UK Ltd.
Milton Keynes UK
UKOW04f2018260115

245158UK00001B/323/P